W9-BBA-821

Bluestem

Frances Arrington

Philomel Books
New York

✿✿✿

To the memory of Nana and chimes
and golden windows

PATRICIA LEE GAUCH, EDITOR

Book design by Sharon Murray Jacobs.
The text is set in 12.5 point Simoncini Garamond.
Library of Congress Cataloging-in-Publication Data
Arrington, Frances.
Bluestem / by Frances Arrington. p. cm.
Summary: With their father away and their mother traumatized
by some unknown event, eleven-year-old Polly and her younger sister
are left to take care of themselves and their prairie homestead.
[1. Sisters—Fiction. 2. Frontier and pioneer life—Fiction. 3. Prairies—Fiction.]
I. Title.
PZ7.A74337 B1 2000
[Fic]—dc21   99-053726
ISBN 0-399-23564-7
3 5 7 9 10 8 6 4

❧ Contents ❧

Acknowledgments

For sharing their knowledge of the tall grass prairies and the people who settled there, I am indebted to: Lisa McMillan, Jerome Lucas, Gerald Jasmer, John Albert, Kimberli Stine, and John Peck of the USDA, Natural Resources Conservation Service in Nebraska; James Stubbendieck and David Wishart of the Center for Great Plains Studies-University of Nebraska; Troy Walz and Dennis Ferraro of the Cooperative Extension Offices-University of Nebraska; Chuck Butterfield and Frederick Luebke of the University of Nebraska; Vern Souder of the Conservation and Survey Division-University of Nebraska; Mike Fritz and John Dinan of the Nebraska Game and Parks Commission; Chris Helzer of the Nature Conservancy-Nebraska; Steve Holland of the Iowa Department of Transportation; Dorothy Schwieder of Iowa State University; Jim Zohrer of the Iowa Department of Natural Resources; Herbert Hoover of the University of South Dakota; Gary Larson of South Dakota State University; Dave Rambo of the Old Court House Museum in Sioux Falls, South Dakota; Mary Landkamer of the Custer County Historical Society; Lowell Soike of the State Historical Society of Iowa; Jack Holzhueter of the Wisconsin State Historical Society; Jim Potter, John Carter, Richard Spencer, and David Murphy of the Nebraska State Historical Society; Tim Terry and Helen Schweizer of the Platte County Historical Society; Kevin Brown of Garfield County Historical Society.

In addition, many thanks to Patricia Lee Gauch.

1

The Waiters

*M*ama loved the flowers. Though she never complained, Mama loved little about the prairie. But she loved the flowers. Indeed that is what she was searching for that day. Some purple coneflowers somewhere east of the creek where they found wild onions once. Polly and Jessie went too, in the wagon. They dangled their bare feet in the tall grasses and watched the sky turn into a storm. . . .

Huge and black and wide, its top edged with stunning white curls, it encircled the western sky. It loomed tall as the stars and black as the night against the deep sunny colors of the wide prairie that spread out before it.

"Look how dark it is, Mama!" Polly said, admiring the storm from the back of the wagon where she sat with Jessie. They turned their faces toward the cold wind and watched the furthermost ridges blacken with the storm's shadow.

"We should go back, shouldn't we, Mama?" said Jessie.

Mama glanced back at the sky then and Polly saw Mama's eyes and wondered at how they seemed to be looking somewhere beyond the sky, past it somehow. Mama shook her head. "We will be safe, I think," she said. "This one, perhaps it will go by to the south." Polly squinted her eyes a little, watching Mama a moment longer before looking back at the sky.

Nonetheless Mama said they could wait at the Smiths' soddy while she gathered her coneflowers. She'd be back soon. They rumbled along, the heavy wagon creaking, nearing the Smiths' homestead. Polly wished she could go on with Mama. *She* was not afraid of storms. But Jessie was. And of people too. So Polly did not complain. Mama left them at the Smiths' soddy. She kissed them on their foreheads and told them not to be any trouble, to wait there.

The storm never came.

Polly and Jessie sat on the hard bench outside

the Smiths' in the wind and the sun, the wind teasing their light hair from underneath the bonnets and whipping it on their faces so that the bonnets were abandoned, and still Mama did not come and still they did not know.

They made up a game, chasing each other a short distance between the soddy and an outbuilding, but Mrs. Smith appeared at the door and looked hard at them. So they stopped and sat on the bench again, the strong wind beating their threadbare dresses against their bare legs and ankles.

Again Mrs. Smith appeared, throwing dishwater from a basin out on the ground just short of their feet. Polly looked over, squinting in the bright sun, and smiled at the tiny boy peeping out from behind Mrs. Smith's skirt. Jessie kept her eyes on the ground in front of her and wished Mrs. Smith would not come out again, wished she was at home.

"How old you girls getting to be now?" Ruth Smith asked.

"I'm eleven," Polly said. "She's nine."

"Your ma 'spect me to feed you two?"

"No, ma'am, she didn't expect you to feed us," offered Polly, still squinting and holding her hand over her eyes.

Ruth Smith sniffed, rubbing her neck.

Polly tried to untangle her face from squinting and smile at Mrs. Smith. "She should be back anytime now."

Jessie raised her eyes and glanced quickly at Ruth Smith. Then her eyes darted back to the ground.

Ruth Smith studied Jessie for a moment. "Mighty sad face, girl," she said, and shaking her head, she disappeared again into the soddy.

Polly looked at Jessie and raised her eyebrows.

"I didn't mean anything. Honest," Jessie said, her eyes troubled and confused.

"I know," Polly said. "It's all right. Don't fret."

Polly frowned and sat staring again over the prairie, searching the horizon for Mama but seeing only the endless waves of grass and the huge sky.

So they waited. The sun was low in the sky. They sat on the bench in front of the Smiths' soddy and watched the sun drop even lower and thought Mama was coming back. They did not know. Even then.

They sat in silence. Raef Smith and Simon and another of the Smiths' older sons, Polly thought he might be named Paul, came in from the oat fields.

Polly hadn't seen any of them since the firebreaks had been burned in the spring. Simon and the other son stabled the team. Raef Smith coughed, spit profusely, and went into the soddy.

Polly and Jessie would have waited longer. They would have if it had not been for the words. Words overheard from inside the soddy. Words not meant for them to hear. Not that they believed the words— the words were not true—but because they could not imagine anyone thinking those words.

Papa didn't leave us, Polly thought. Papa would never leave us. And Mama. Mama *is* coming back.

Polly would not stay here. She would not stay here one minute longer. She stood and went to the door that led into the dark hovel.

She waited until Raef Smith looked up and saw her there.

"Excuse me, Mr. Smith, Mrs. Smith. We're leaving now. Mama comes by, please tell her we went on home."

The Smiths looked at Polly. Polly hesitated. "And my papa . . . my papa's leg got broke . . . a horse bolted. That's why he's not back. He went to bury his brother . . . my uncle . . ." Polly stopped herself. They knew. They knew about Papa's brother dying in Fort Randall. Cholera. All of it. Mama had told them.

"And Papa . . . he's bringing wood for this winter too, from the river valley east of there . . . on the way back." They know it's a long trip, Polly thought, and hard this time especially.

She was talking too much. She knew it. She couldn't help herself. "But he'll be back soon as his leg mends. You'll see." Polly kept on. "And Mama's just late. So we're going on now."

Polly took Jessie's arm and started to back away.

"Your ma ain't comin', girl. The sun's most ready to set . . ." Raef Smith began.

"Hush, Raef," said Mrs. Smith. "Let 'em go." She looked back at the girls. "We'll tell your ma."

The girls left, walking into a prairie darkening quickly with the coming twilight. The wind cooled and pushed the loose hair off their faces. They walked silently, glancing back at the tiny light from inside the Smiths' soddy, the little blackening silhouettes of the Smiths' stables, and the waves and waves of grass.

And still they did not know.

"How can we find the way in the dark?" Jessie was whining.

Polly didn't like it when Jessie whined. Nine years old is too old to whine, she thought. Jessie had stopped walking. She was standing on one bare foot, the other one pulled up behind her, her head twisted backwards in an effort to examine a cut. There was sharp grass stubble from a prairie fire in the spring and it hurt their feet.

"Come *on,*" Polly said. "We're almost to the ridge top."

"But how can we find our way?" Jessie continued, following Polly's example and taking long strides through the tall grasses. "What if we get lost?"

"We won't get lost."

Mama wasn't coming anyway. Something had happened to her. They came to a plowed field and followed the long turns of rich, black loam the rest of the way to the ridge top and the road, what little there was of it, just ruts made by wagon wheels. There was still light but the eastern sky was dark.

"Stars are coming out," said Polly. "It'll be all right. We'll be able to see fine." She slapped the tall grasses out of her way and Jessie followed behind her. They loved the stars and the night and the prairie winds and the grass that went on and on to the sky. But now they were afraid. They walked on in the quiet. Dusk became night.

"Look, there's the claim stake. We'll just follow the ridge and be home in no time," Polly said.

Jessie hurried to keep up.

"Mama just got held up. Something like a broken axle. She'll get home sometime tonight or by morning surely," Polly told Jessie.

And herself.

2

The Rocker

They found their way home covering two miles on foot. They found their way home to their small, dark soddy not far from the creek bottoms. Their small, dark home with no light in the window.

Helga was mooing near the stable. Jessie said she'd see to her and the calf. Polly went into the cool soddy. Her hands felt their way on the wall to the peg the kerosene lamp hung on, her eyes adjusting to the dark.

Someone was there already . . . inside the soddy . . . someone whose eyes had already adjusted to the dark. But Polly didn't know. Polly didn't see them. There was a still glow in the room when Polly put down the lamp. She went to the stove, found the iron and kindling and caught a tiny flicker on the twisted grass. There, she thought, watching the fire and resting on the stool. When the fire was steady, she lit the smaller lamp thinking Jessie would need it in the stable. And she added more cobs to the fire, glad to be home, glad she wasn't waiting anymore at the Smiths'. Waiting here would be better.

And someone was there all the while.

When the fire was burning steady, Polly put the lantern on the sideboard and lifted the skillet to start supper.

And then she heard something . . . just a small sound. Something was moving inside the soddy. To her left. In the dark. She stood still. Her hands gripped the heavy skillet. She wanted to put it down but she didn't want to move. Her eyes searched the dark room. The chair was moving. There was someone in the chair. In the rocker. Polly's eyes shot toward the door, then back to the chair. She felt her throat getting tight, beginning to hurt. She heard the clock ticking and the wind rattling the open door.

It was a woman.

Mama?

She heard a little murmur come from herself. Was it Mama?

Take the lamp. Say something. See who it is, she thought.

But she stood still where she was, her hands unwilling to let go of the heavy skillet, her mouth open, breathing and staring wide-eyed at the woman in the rocking chair over by the bed. Polly swallowed. A quick movement, a rat, across the floor, distracted her eyes again and the figure remained in the chair. And Polly stood alone in her soddy. And there was a figure in the chair.

"Mama?" she said softly, her voice breaking. It couldn't be Mama though, she thought. Just sitting there rocking. Saying nothing.

Sammy strolled in the door. Polly could hear his loud purr. Oh, Sammy, she thought. Then Jessie came. "Helga was so . . ." Jessie stopped, puzzled by the lost look she saw on her sister's face, and Jessie turned and then she saw too.

"Mama?" Jessie breathed. "Mama," she said out loud.

The figure moved. Just a deep breath.

"Mama," Polly repeated.

Polly snatched the lamp from the sideboard, and hurried to the chair.

"Mama, what happened? You scared us." Polly

set the lamp on the pine plank table almost toppling it in her eagerness, and smiled, breathing deeply again. "We came on home ourselves. It was . . . " Her voice trailed off as she looked into her mother's face.

Mama didn't hear them.

They searched Mama's face, watched her in silent bewilderment.

And then Jessie's voice pierced the silence. "Something's wrong with her!" It was almost a scream. She grabbed Polly's arm and pulled on it.

Polly stooped in front of the chair, placed her hands over Mama's on the armrests. "Mama!?" Polly began. It was hard to breathe. "What's wrong, Mama!"

"Why won't she talk!" Jessie moaned. "Why didn't you come for us, Mama? We were scared. . . ." Jessie stood squeezing one hand in the other.

Polly stood up, her eyes searching Mama's empty ones, and Polly's eyes shone with a building terror. She had seen this before. Once, outside of Fort Dodge, she had seen this. A woman inside a covered wagon. Papa was talking to the man who was driving and Polly had been walking by their own wagon and she had seen the woman. A woman who just sat. Just stared. Polly had said hello. The woman had not looked at her, had not heard her. And now Mama did not look, did not hear.

Jessie came forward hesitantly, knelt by the chair, began asking Mama to talk, asking what was wrong, softly pleading with her now. The same things, over and over and over. And Polly watched. She twisted her braid in her fingers and watched. And all she could think was that she wasn't ready. She wasn't ready for this.

Don't be this way, Mama . . .

She wanted to run from the room, and for a moment she thought she would, but suddenly she felt sick. She backed away. Backed away to the iron stove, stooped down and sat on the stool there.

"Polly?" It was Jessie, turning to her. Jessie, wanting to know what to do. "Polly?" Polly wanted to run but Jessie was there. She made herself stay put.

"She doesn't hear you, Jessie," said Polly. Her voice was almost a whisper. Chill bumps rose on her skin. She rubbed her arms. Jessie turned to Polly, and then back to Mama. They waited in silence, and listened to Sammy's purring and the rattle of the door prodded by the wind.

In the quiet they heard the soft whinny of a horse.

"Gus," Polly said softly, suddenly remembering the horse. Mama had left the Smiths' with the horse and wagon. Polly hadn't given a thought to Gus.

"I'll get him." Polly picked up the kerosene lamp. She left Jessie and Mama and ran out through the wild grasses to find the horse.

Around the side of the stable, Polly saw Gus still hitched to the wagon, the great Belgian horse waiting quietly a few yards south of the corncrib.

"Poor boy," she said, loosening the harness, unhitching him from the wagon and patting him on his neck. "Poor Gus. How long have you been waiting out here, hmmm? Come on." Polly led the old horse to the stable and got the currycomb.

Her mama would never have done this. Mama, always so kind to the animals. She rubbed the horse down, watered him, put him in his stall.

Mama *did* forget to do things after the baby died last winter, and when little Karl died the winter before. And she wouldn't eat. But Papa had gotten Mama to eat. And she had. She had eaten a little for Papa. And now Papa was gone. Polly gave Gus one last pat on his strong neck and ran back to the soddy.

She stopped in the door. "Maybe Mama'll eat something . . ." she said.

She turned then and checked the flames. "I'll get the corn cakes we had left over this morning . . . we should eat," Polly said, her voice fading away to a whisper.

Jessie looked around. Her voice shook. "*You* eat," she said.

Polly looked over at Jessie. Jessie was glaring at her. "There's nothing we can do," Polly said. She went to a large jar and took out the leftover corn cakes. "We'll have these and milk. You get the milk, please, Jessie. And I'll warm these."

Jessie glared at her. Polly looked away and went to get the pail herself.

"We have to *do something!*" screamed Jessie.

"What? What are we going to do?" Polly screamed back, and Sammy crouched down low on the dirt floor and scooted under the bed. "Now look what you did." Polly followed Sammy to the bed, got down on her knees and looked under, then sat up, still kneeling, looking at Jessie.

"We *have* to do *something*," Jessie said again. Not screaming anymore. Tears welling up in her eyes. They looked at Mama.

"It's like that woman in Fort Dodge. Remember?" Polly said. Jessie didn't answer.

Polly remembered. Some people lost their minds.

3

The Letter

From under the covers of her bed at daybreak Polly studied Mama. Surely when she got up, Mama would look her way and say something. Or maybe just smile. So Polly took a careful breath and got up slowly, glancing at Mama all the while, and stood waiting on the cool, earthen floor.

"Mama," she whispered and she stood and waited in the quiet. She heard something behind her, and saw it was Jessie leaning up on both arms watching too.

"Are you feeling better this morning, Mama?" Polly glanced back nervously at Jessie as she spoke and then again at Mama.

Nothing.

"It's morning, Mama," she said, trying again.

But no . . . Mama was the same.

Polly stood there, frozen with that truth. She heard her own breath coming quickly in short little bursts. They were alone.

She lingered there until the panic swept over her and was gone. She glanced back at Jessie again and said nothing. She hoped Jessie would not start whining and crying and making things worse.

Jessie was watching her, waiting to see what she was going to do.

She would get breakfast, they would do their chores, milk Helga, grind some corn, take water to the chickens. The everyday things. She would get breakfast. Because everything inside her still wanted to run. She wanted to run out on the prairie, all the way up to the ridge top, and when she could run no longer she wanted to drop to the ground and stay there and only then would she turn and look back. From a distance.

Polly dressed and picked up a twisted clump of grass she would use to start up the flames in the stove.

And Jessie, still in her nightgown, got busy sprinkling salt on the floor.

"You're putting too much," Polly said.

"Mama likes it."

Polly looked over at the chair where Mama still sat rocking ever so slightly. She looked back at Jessie and then at the dirt floor. The salt made it stay hard so they could sweep it easily. And Mama liked a clean floor.

"Just don't waste that salt, Jessie," Polly said. "You don't want to run out. It'll be a while yet 'fore Papa gets back."

Jessie's eyes searched Polly's face and she continued. "We have enough. Maybe it'll help her feel better," she told Polly.

Polly frowned. If Papa were back . . .

"I'll write Papa today," Polly said. Then turning to Mama, added, "Mama? I'm going to write Papa . . . he'll come on back early. Papa'll come . . ." But Mama wasn't listening.

We are still here, Mama.

Polly went to the door and opened it. The warm air outside pushed into the cool of the soddy. Polly ran to the stable, led Gus out and turned him loose. He began to graze and she ran out past Papa's new fields into the edge of the vast prairie. She stopped, and even then the grasses slapped against her arms and legs and the strong wind rushed on across the rolling prairie. This is where she would spend the whole day every day if she only could, watching its skies and birds. The whole day, watching the deep soft colors of the grasses. Colors that changed from the clouds passing over them and from the land that folded below them.

Because she was the oldest, she told herself, she had to be brave. That's what Papa would do, she told herself. But she didn't feel brave. She swallowed hard, pressed her lips tightly together, and turned back to the soddy.

Standing in the doorway, Polly watched Jessie on the stool in front of Mama, telling Mama about the Smiths' hog, how it had run from them.

"Polly said, 'Hello, Piggy,' to it and started saying 'souey souey' and introduced herself and it looked shocked . . ." Jessie giggled, and Polly hugged her arms.

Look at her, Mama. She wants you to laugh.

Yet Mama sat, her head tilted over just a little, her blue eyes open and vacant.

". . . and the squeal, Mama," Jessie continued. "You should have heard it. Polly can squeal just like their pig, she did on the way home. Get her to do it for you, Mama. It's so funny." Jessie laughed and then just as suddenly the laugh was gone. Jessie knew Mama wasn't listening. And Jessie's face fell. She stood up and waited by the rocker, her face as blank as Mama's, and Polly backed against the door frame.

Mama started rocking again, staring straight ahead, and the wind blew in the door and moved her hair.

Polly wrote two letters. The first one she tore up and threw into the ashes because she thought of Papa. She could see his smile when he got the letter, and could see his face fall like Jessie's had done the morning he opened it and began to read about Mama. She did not want him to get that letter, so now it burned slowly behind the little iron door of the stove and Polly stared in at the flames and watched the paper curl and turn black and dissolve into cinders.

And then a noise startled her. It was just Sammy jumping down from the bed. Polly watched him go over to Mama in the chair and purr and rub up against her leg and Polly knew she *had* to write the letter to Papa. So she began again.

Dear Papa,

I hope your leg is healing fine. Jessie and I are well, but Mama isn't. She left us at the Smiths' yesterday and didn't come for us. When we got home we found her here, but she doesn't know us. Mostly she just sits in the rocker and stares. She'll go with Jessie to the outhouse, and when we told her it was time to wash from the basin, she did. But she won't talk. She eats some. We gave her some corn cakes and milk last night. We were surprised that she ate it.

Jessie and I will be all right by ourselves till you get back. Can it be soon? We'll take care of the stock and the garden. Please write us back and tell us if there's something we should do about Mama. We don't know what to do.

Love, Polly

Polly looked at the letter. It didn't tell everything. It didn't tell how last night she sat on the side of their trundle bed and watched in silence while Jessie tried to get Mama to talk, the same begging, the same questions, again and again. Why hadn't she come back to the Smiths'? What had happened? Why wouldn't she talk? Over and over and over.

And it didn't tell how Polly had wondered *when* Jessie would stop her questions and *why* she wouldn't stop. Or how she herself sat there and waited. Her hands folded in her lap. Her hair falling in her face. Watching. She didn't say that in the letter.

And she didn't say that she felt like screaming at Jessie to stop begging like that because Mama wasn't going to talk. She was quiet. And just waited. Finally Jessie did stop pleading with Mama. And Polly stopped waiting. They were too tired. They fell asleep and slept through the rest of the night, while Mama sat in the rocking chair and rocked.

4

The Carrier

When the letter was done, Polly and Gus followed the little road along the ridge tops to the Smiths' homestead, carrying the letter to Papa, and Polly decided she would not tell the Smiths about what had happened to Mama, no matter what. She would never tell them. The Smiths had thought, they had *said* Papa and Mama had left them. It was a lie. You were supposed to forgive your enemies. Mama had read it to her in the Book of Matthew and she would try to forgive them . . . for saying those things . . . even if they *didn't* think she had heard. But she wasn't ready to yet.

And then she knew that part of it was not really a lie. Not really a lie after all. Not the part about

Mama. Mama *had* left them. It was true what the Smiths had said yesterday.

Only yesterday, but a lifetime ago.

Gus moved along the crest of the ridge without guidance from Polly. And the wind that had been just a whisper earlier became steady and strong.

When she was still a half mile off she could make out someone near the outbuildings past the prairie grasses and oats and cornfields.

In the spring, with Papa, she had come here. The Smiths' plowshare had snapped. Her papa had brought his steel plowshare and Gus and the two new young horses. He had helped, turning up the heavy sod with Raef Smith and his two older sons to make up for time lost.

Other days she had come here with Mama. "Come, Polly! Jessie!" Mama would say. "The hens have been busy. Perhaps our neighbors would like much some of so many eggs?" Polly knew that what Mama really meant was she felt so alone out on the homestead, so away from the rest of the world that she'd settle for a short visit. Even if it was a visit with Ruth Smith.

There wasn't anyone else. People, the Roberts,

the Millers, others, had just begun to settle in when the grasshoppers had come. Now their claims lay abandoned, their drooping soddies almost lost in the bluestem and Indian grass. So now Ruth Smith was the only other woman for most twenty miles.

Polly found her at the clothesline, the tiny boy playing on the ground underneath. She slid off Gus.

"Morning, Mrs. Smith," she said, shielding her eyes from the sun with her hand.

Ruth Smith looked Polly up and down. "Morning," she said, and went back to hanging the clothes on the line. She gave Polly a hard look, like she wanted to say something. But she said nothing.

"If Mr. Smith could mail this for us next time he's in Arcadia, we'd be grateful," Polly said, squinting at Mrs. Smith, her loose hair flying in the wind. Arcadia was almost thirty miles away but had the nearest post office.

"What makes you scrunch your face up so, girl?"

"It's just the sun, it hurts my eyes," Polly answered. "And it makes 'em water some. That's all."

Ruth Smith stared at Polly. Polly gave her a little smile, remembering to be courteous.

"You need to get that hair out of your eyes, girl."

"Yes, ma'am," said Polly, pushing at her long bangs.

"Your ma come home?" Mrs. Smith asked, frowning at Polly.

"Yes, ma'am."

Mrs. Smith raised her eyebrows. Polly waited, pushing her hair behind her ears.

"Is Mr. Smith going for mail anytime soon?"

"Can't say. Soon enough, I guess." Ruth Smith shook a shirt at Polly. Polly stepped back.

"Here's the money for the post," said Polly, frowning at the coin in her hand. It had come dear and she wished she could mail the letter herself . . . could go to town . . . somehow. She glanced back at Mrs. Smith, who took the coin, put it in her apron with the letter. Polly stood looking at her. She tried to look pleasant and smile again, but her face ached so from the bright sun and she figured Mrs. Smith would not find it to her liking under any circumstances.

"Thank you," she said, backing away. "Bye, little boy." She took another step backwards and then turned and ran back to Gus.

She took her bonnet, which hung from her neck, and put it on, though it was little help to her eyes against the glaring sun. She started for home, look-ing across the miles and miles of grass. A sea of grass, Papa had told her the first homesteaders had called it. It rolled on and on as far as the eye could see, rolling in waves pushed by the wind. And where there wasn't grass, there was sky. Polly followed a hawk into the tumbling piles of clouds.

She hoped the Smiths would mail the letter soon, so Papa would still be at Fort Randall to get it. She thought about Papa. Maybe he too was some-where thinking about hawks in flight and waves of grass and skies full of wind.

5

The Promise

When Polly got to where she could see the soddy, she jumped off Gus and began to walk. From the ridge, she looked across the wild grasses to the north. North was where Papa would come from. Across hills and tablelands and ridges, across a hundred miles was Papa.

Polly looked toward the soddy. She didn't want to go back. She didn't want to go in. Not with Mama in there like she was. The new Mama. The one with the empty eyes. Eyes she did not know. Polly raced down along the edge of the barley fields, stopping out of breath just before she got to the stable.

Turning back to Gus, she watched the old horse run along the same path she had taken, running to her, his hooves upturning sod, his long mane and tail tossing gently. She reached up and smoothed his golden mane as he came to a stop.

She led him to the stable and got the currycomb and the soft brush she would need to rub him down.

Jessie had followed her.

"Did they say when they'd mail the letter?" Jessie asked, standing in the doorway.

Polly looked around and saw Jessie nervously picking at the tie around the end of her long braid. Gus tossed his head and Polly turned back to brushing his shoulder.

"Did they?" said Jessie, coming closer.

"No. But Mrs. Smith said it would be soon."

"I wonder what Papa will do when he gets the letter . . . about Mama, I mean," said Jessie.

Polly stopped brushing and looked at Jessie. What *would* Papa do about Mama? Send her back to visit her family in the old country where maybe she'd get better? Could Papa get money for that? Mama missed the beautiful land where she had been born. Polly knew. Mama never said so but Polly knew. Mama missed it there the same as Polly would miss these grasslands if she left them.

But Papa could never get money for that. The money Papa had saved was gone now, used up when the grasshoppers came. After the babies Papa had told Mama how they would save every bit they could and after the title was clear, they would sell the farm and move to a place Mama would like better. After the babies he had told Mama that.

"I don't know what he'll do," Polly said.

"He'll just come home soon as he gets it," Jessie said after a moment. She went to Gus's face and stood stroking his head and Polly started brushing Gus's side again, smoothing his shiny coat with her hand.

"And then . . ." Jessie looked over at Polly quickly, her eyes brighter. "And then Mama'll be better, you think?"

"Maybe," Polly said quietly. *Maybe nothing would help.* The thought squeezed out of Polly's mind along with the beginning of tears and she brushed them all away. Yes, it would help Mama when Papa got back. Of course it would.

"I'm hungry," Jessie continued. She twirled the string around the end of her braid. "I dug three potatoes and some turnips and washed them."

"That's good. We can have them with biscuits for supper."

Mama wouldn't eat the biscuits and turnips. They were good biscuits, thought Polly as she laid the washed dishes in the cupboard. They were the best biscuits I ever made. Why couldn't she eat them?

She went to the sideboard, took the framed photograph off the marble top, and sat on the stool by the stove looking at it. The frame was sterling silver from Sweden. The photograph was of Papa and Mama, Elsa and herself. Polly was only three in the photograph. It was taken before they moved to this prairie, when they still lived in Iowa.

Papa and Mama sat so straight in two chairs, side by side in the picture. If you looked very close you could see the coral comb holding up Mama's hair. The comb Papa had given her. Mama looks so young, thought Polly. Polly couldn't remember Mama looking so young like that.

And then there was Elsa. She had died when Polly had just turned six. And Mama couldn't stay there anymore after Elsa died. They had left the homestead in Iowa and come here. Polly looked at Elsa's round eyes. She looked like me, Polly thought. She wished Elsa had lived, and that she was there with them now. And she wished her two baby brothers had lived too. She thought of the two small crosses not far from the soddy where they were buried, little Patrik not more than a year ago, and she felt the tears pushing at her eyes.

Polly bit her lip. She wouldn't think about the babies. She *wouldn't.*

She turned around and looked at Jessie. Jessie was brushing Mama's hair. "Polly wrote a letter to Papa today," Jessie said to Mama. "When Papa gets it, he'll come back then. And Polly told Papa we'd be all right till he comes."

While Jessie braided Mama's hair and pinned it up, Polly looked again at the photograph and watched the lamp flicker lightly on the silver frame and thought about her letter.

It was kind of like a promise, her letter. A promise to Papa. And a promise to Jessie. That they'd be all right till Papa came. And while she had not realized it at the time, she had made that promise when she wrote the letter.

Days passed. Mama rocked, seldom leaving the chair, eating little, responding to the children only when urged to eat or wash or go to the outhouse. But never a word. Never a word to Polly and Jessie.

And Polly and Jessie went on. They cooked and mucked out the stable and carried laundry through the wet meadows, through the slough, running alongside the creek that fed into the river a mile north of the homestead.

And Polly thought often of the promise she had made. The promise she was determined to keep.

6

The Trespasser

*H*ere, Mama," Polly said. Six days and still Mama sat in the rocker and Polly tried to get Mama to take the plate. "We made these for your breakfast. You need to eat more."

They were the best corn cakes. The ones that weren't burned around the edges like the ones she and Jessie had eaten. Mama wouldn't take the corn cakes. Polly turned away. She left the corn cakes on the table and ran out to the stable where she sat tracing the wood grain on the smooth, warm bench there. She remembered Papa making the bench out of an old wagon plank. She looked to the horizon, searching for Papa. It had been more than three weeks since Papa left. If he hadn't gotten hurt, they would have expected him back today. Then it occurred to her.

Maybe *Papa* had written a letter and sent it on ahead telling *them* when they could expect him home. Maybe when the Smiths had gone to mail her letter they had picked up Papa's! It would be one he wrote before he could have gotten theirs. Still there would be news. Maybe even news of when he would come home.

So after they mucked out the stable and picked some snap beans and laid beans they had shelled yesterday out to dry between sheets on top of the corncrib, and after Polly made dinner for later, she and Jessie went on Gus to the Smiths' homestead to see if there was a letter from Papa.

"Will she be mad?" Jessie asked.

"She might," Polly said. "But . . . I'm going. Anyway."

Ruth Smith came outside as the girls rode up.

Polly jumped down. "Morning, Mrs. Smith." She tried to smile. She needn't have bothered.

"Something wrong?" Ruth Smith frowned.

"We came to see if Mr. Smith's been to Arcadia yet. We thought there might have been a letter . . ." Polly hesitated.

"This is a homestead, girl. Plenty to keep us busy enough without running a letter over to the Johansson girls the minute Raef's back."

"Oh no, ma'am. I never meant . . . that's why I came, to pick up any letter . . . if there was one," Polly said. She wished she hadn't smiled.

Polly shifted from foot to foot. She looked expectantly at Mrs. Smith.

Mrs. Smith looked up at Jessie. "And you're looking for a letter too?" she said. Jessie smiled but her eyes dropped when they caught Ruth Smith's and she fingered the reins nervously.

"Can't speak?" Ruth Smith continued. Jessie opened her mouth and glanced up again but again her eyes dropped in painful silence.

"She's shy when she's not 'round her kin," Polly said, quickly looking back at Jessie. Jessie glanced again at Mrs. Smith, then Polly, her face beginning to burn at the words.

"No excuse for not answerin' when spoken to." Mrs. Smith lifted her chin, looking at Polly.

Polly winced under the critical gaze. "She's real shy."

"Your ma's the same?" asked Mrs. Smith.

"The same?" Polly said slowly. The same as

what? Polly's heart began to race. *The Smiths had read her letter?* Ruth Smith said nothing, just looked hard at Polly.

"Weren't no mail for you, girl," Mrs. Smith said abruptly, and turned to go back inside.

"So Mr. Smith has been?" Polly said, brightening. At least her letter was in the mail! "When did he go?"

Mrs. Smith turned back again and looked at Polly, saying nothing.

"So as I could know when my letter got mailed, ma'am. Then I could figure on when it'd get there. That's all I meant. Didn't mean any harm."

"Didn't I tell you I've got things to do?" Mrs. Smith said.

Polly stood and tried to remember something about not speaking in anger. Something Mama had read to her from Proverbs. She couldn't remember.

Ruth Smith turned to go back down in the soddy.

Polly looked back at Jessie, bewildered.

"Let's just go, Polly," Jessie whispered, leaning forward, her eyes pleading.

But Polly asked again, "Mrs. Smith? When did he go?" That's all she wanted to know.

Ruth Smith shook her head, looked first at Polly, then Jessie, and back at Polly before she spoke.

"Middle of last week," she said. "Now you girls go on." And Ruth Smith disappeared into her soddy, leaving Polly standing and staring at the door.

"Mrs. Smith," she called. She peered into the door of the soddy and saw Mrs. Smith come near the door. It was dark inside and Polly could barely see her.

"Listen here, child. You go on home. I've got work to do," Mrs. Smith said.

Polly stood in her sleeveless long dress squinting at the vague figure inside the dark doorway. She heard the cotton dress whipping about her legs in the wind. She bit her lips, turned, and walked back to Jessie and the horse.

The girls rode away, Gus's slow, sure feet walking through the grass, carrying them home. But Polly kept looking back, watching the horizon to see when the Smiths' soddy was out of sight.

"Whoa," she murmured. "Get down, Jessie."

The horse stopped and they jumped down. Jessie stood holding the reins. She followed Polly's gaze back toward the Smiths'.

"Why did she say that? About Mama. 'Was she the same?' She must've read our letter. She must've, Jessie! Maybe Mr. Smith hasn't even been to town. Maybe they still have our letter," said Polly. She sighed, and looked back. "What should we do?"

"We should go home. Let's just go home."

Polly's eyes stayed on the grasses dancing atop the swell of prairie behind which lay the Smiths' soddy. Her lips rubbed nervously back and forth across themselves, and her eyes squinted in the bright sun.

"No," she said. "No, I want to know they mailed our letter."

Jessie dropped her shoulders. Her eyes wandered again in the direction Polly was looking.

"You wait here," Polly said slowly. "You just wait. I'm going back, but I won't let them see me."

"No!" Jessie gasped.

"I'll be careful. I want to know. I have to know," Polly said. "I'll go back and if she leaves the house, maybe I can get in and see. If they still have our letter and if they opened it."

"No, Polly. Let's just go home."

"You wait here."

Jessie stood holding Gus's reins tightly and watched Polly leave. Polly crept through the grasses and came up over a low hill back of the soddy where a rail fence enclosed three graves. She stared at the crosses for a moment as she crouched there waiting. She had heard Papa mention the Smith children that died. Pneumonia. Fevers. The Smiths too had known sorrow.

Her chance came. Mrs. Smith went to the garden. Polly scrambled down the slope and into the dark opening of the soddy. Her eyes darted about on the sideboard to the oil paper in one of the windows, the cupboard, the shelves. A side of bacon hung from the willow rafters above her head alongside dried vegetables. She saw an apron hanging on a peg. The same apron Mrs. Smith had put the letter in five days ago. Polly shot to it, her hands searching the pocket. Nothing. She put the apron back carefully, turned, and then her eyes fell on an envelope. It was stuffed behind an iron kettle on the cupboard. She took it.

It was her letter, the envelope open, the letter inside. She glanced back at the door. The bright glare of the sun hurt her eyes. Her hands searched around the kettle. The money was gone.

"What're you doin' here? You thievin', girl?" Simon Smith's voice filled the room. Simon was only three years older than her, but he was almost as big as his father. Then she saw Raef Smith coming toward her. She looked up at him, her eyes wide and her mouth agape. In her hand she held the letter.

"What you got in that hand?" he said. She could see the whiskers on his face. "Open your hand." Polly looked at the letter, her hand opened, and the letter fell on the dirt floor. Backing away, she stumbled, caught her balance, and stopped. She heard Simon laugh.

"It's my letter!" she suddenly screamed. "It's open!"

Ruth Smith had appeared at the door with the small boy in tow. "What's she doing in here?"

"Caught her poking around. Tryin' to steal? You think?" Raef said.

"I wasn't stealing!" Polly's words came tumbling out. "I didn't take anything. I only came to see if you'd mailed my letter. You said you had but here it is!"

"I told you Raef went to Arcadia last week. Never said he mailed your letter. Turns out he left it here, forgot it."

"It's open. Why did you open it?" Polly cried. "And where is the money I gave you to mail it?"

"Don't you raise your voice to me."

Polly closed her mouth and stared. Ruth Smith went to a glass jar stuffed behind a jumble of other jars in a small cabinet. "The money's gone . . . and more'n her post."

Polly stared in disbelief at her.

"Well, I guess it ain't too hard to figure out where it flew off to," Raef said.

Polly started backing up again. "I didn't take it!" she shouted. Surprised at herself, she lowered her voice. "I'm sorry I came in your house. I am. But I didn't take it!"

"You'll be owin' us, girl."

"I don't have it," Polly said. Her mind raced. Mrs. Smith must have taken it herself or maybe Simon . . . Polly looked around at Simon, then back at Mrs. Smith. "Someone knows!" Polly gasped.

Mrs. Smith's eyes narrowed. "You think 'cause your ma's not looking, you can just go off prowling in our house? Your ma teach you that?"

Raef Smith watched Polly sidle backwards until she tripped and fell onto the dirt floor, her hands behind her.

"You ever let me catch you in my house again . . ." he said.

Polly grabbed the letter, got to her feet, and stumbled from the soddy. She ran without looking back, reached Jessie and fell to her knees. She turned up the bottom of her bare foot, pushing at a cut with her thumb. It wasn't that bad.

"What happened?" Jessie asked, wide-eyed. Polly opened her hand and showed Jessie the crumpled letter. Jessie picked it up and held it.

"Our letter?" she asked. "They had our letter." Her voice trailed off. She unfolded it carefully and it trembled in the breeze.

And Polly wondered if she hadn't gone looking, if she hadn't gone in their house, whether maybe they might have gotten around to mailing it. Maybe. But not now. Not after what she did. Now there was no chance.

And she hated the Smiths. All of them. Except that tiny boy. It was hard to be a Christian around them.

"Let's go ourselves! Let's go and mail it ourselves, Polly!" Jessie said, her voice frantic. "On Gus."

"Thirty miles? . . . And leave Mama alone all that time. We can't do that, Jessie . . . we can't do that . . ."

The children sat in the middle of the prairie and looked at the letter quivering in Jessie's hands. And they knew that Papa would never read that letter. Papa would not know what had happened until he came back.

7

The Speaker

*P*olly wrote a new letter to Papa to give to a traveler who might happen by one day. She left it in the cupboard knowing a traveler so far out on the prairie would be long in the coming. Now she sat on the stool by the stove twisting prairie grass for kindling while Jessie brought in the milk.

She had been over and over in her mind the happenings at the Smiths' the day before. She was tired of fretting over it.

"Not a lot of milk, she was kind of dry," Jessie said, putting the pail on the table.

"Not a lot of milk . . ."

For a moment they didn't know it was Mama, it came so unexpectedly. They turned to look and

Jessie started toward her. And Mama looked at Jessie.

Mama saw Jessie.

Mama started to say something. She put her hands up toward Jessie, her fingers reaching toward Jessie's face, and started to say something again, stopped, and looked hard at Jessie.

"Mama?" Jessie began to smile, flashed eager eyes at Polly and back again at Mama.

Polly stood holding the twisted grass in both hands, afraid to move, afraid to break the spell, and her own smile came. Mama was back! Her *real* mama was back!

"Mama?" Jessie said again.

"Inga? What are you doing here, Inga?" Mama said.

Inga.

Mama's older sister, Inga. Jessie favored Inga. Mama had told them.

No, no, Mama. Polly waited in the stillness, her eyes blinking, watching to see what might happen next. She wasn't ready. So she waited.

She let the grass fall from her hands to the floor.

"It's Jessie, Mama . . ." Polly began. "Jessie . . ."

Her lips trembled. She bit them. She wanted to run. She wanted to run from this. She looked at her little sister standing by her mama. She made herself stay.

Polly went to Mama, put her hand on Mama's forehead, pushed back some loose hairs, straightening Mama's hair.

"Mama? It's me. And Jessie's here. Jessie's here. Mama? And Papa . . . he'll be coming soon. It can't be much longer. You'll be so glad when he gets back, won't you?" Mama was looking at Polly, seemed to be listening. "I know I sure will be glad when he gets back, won't you? You'll feel better then, won't you?" Polly continued.

"Will he bring my babies?"

Polly's breath pushed in her chest like she'd been hit there. It *was* the babies. She'd been right. Mama was sitting forward in the chair, staring at her. Frantic eyes. Not Mama's eyes.

"Will he?" Mama asked again.

Polly felt her heart skip and then it pounded inside her, inside her neck, inside her ears.

"Will he?" Mama demanded this time. Her eyes locked on Polly's.

"Yes . . ." Polly said. She hadn't known she was

going to say it. "Yes . . ." she said again. And Mama's brows furrowed slightly and she sank back into the chair, looked across the room. Her face blank again. Gone again.

Tears pooled in Polly's eyes. She looked back to Jessie. Jessie had backed away to the bed, was sitting on it, her eyes brimming with tears too. Just tears at first and then her shoulders shook with silent sobs. And she began to cry aloud, like she had as a small child, louder and louder.

"We're gonna be all right, Jessie," Polly said, wiping her cheeks with her hands and sitting down by her sister. "Papa'll come soon. It's true." Jessie leaned into Polly's shoulder and sobbed for a moment, but in a second she was scurrying to Mama, standing by her.

"Why doesn't she know us?" she sobbed, looking back and forth from Mama to Polly. "Why doesn't she get better?" Jessie was shaking, still standing stiffly beside Mama, holding her arms and trembling.

"Papa's coming," Polly told her. "Before we know it, he'll be back."

"I want him now!" Jessie shouted through her sobs.

Polly stared at her. She was acting like a baby. She was too old to be acting that way.

"*When?*" Jessie insisted. "*When* will he get here? I want him *now,*" she cried loudly, as if shouting would make Mama come out of it, would make Papa return.

"Stop it, Jessie!" Polly shouted. "Stop it . . ." she repeated quietly.

Jessie did stop and came back to sit on the bed and began to cry softly.

Polly put her arm around her little sister. "Papa's coming . . ." Polly whispered. And she looked back at Mama. Mama. Rocking in the rocker. Ever so slightly, and staring with vacant eyes up to the dark corners of the room.

"We can wait a little bit longer for Papa. I can. . . . Can you, Jessie?"

Polly heard one of the chickens scratching just out the door. There were chores to do. But she stayed, sitting there on the bed holding her sister, and watched the small lamp across the room. Just stared into the small flames. And over on the marble, Papa and the young mama sat in the straight chairs and looked at her and Jessie and the new mama solemnly from their safe frozen place in the photograph.

8

The Taker

Mama didn't say anything else that day or the next. And yet Polly kept hoping. She would rather have a mama who talked to a sister in Sweden than one who said nothing. A mama who talked to a sister in Sweden was a mama who maybe would come back.

Mama slept in the bed that night after she spoke and the next night too. Jessie had asked her if she wanted to lie down and she had willingly come and slept there next to Jessie, lying under the quilt in her long-sleeved cotton dress with the pearly buttons all the way up the front.

Now she was up again, back in the rocker. And Jessie was talking to her. Talking and fixing her hair, careful to plait it just right and wind it up and pin it into a smooth knot at the back of Mama's head.

Polly held three eggs in her hands. She looked at them for a moment before taking them to Mama and putting one in her hands. "See the fine eggs your hens are laying, Mama." Mama didn't look at Polly, didn't look at the egg. It rolled from her hand, fell to the floor before Polly could catch it, and lay there broken.

So they went on with breakfast and tended the animals. They cleaned the lamps and got dried corn from the corncrib and ground it into cornmeal.

In two more weeks the corn Papa had planted for them and the animals would need picking. After lunch the girls made preserves. They had helped Mama make them last summer.

It was a long afternoon and they were glad when they were finished. Glad that at least Mama had spoken. Glad that the Smiths were leaving them alone. Polly sat on the bed rubbing Sammy under his chin.

"Let me have him. He likes to be rocked," said Jessie, taking Sammy in her arms.

"He does not!" And Polly laughed. It was just

a little laugh, but it surprised her because since Mama had been this way, Polly hadn't laughed. She watched as Sammy hissed and wriggled away from Jessie and she laughed again.

"He hissed at Jessie, Mama," Polly said, scooping Sammy up from the floor and sitting on the bed and laying him in her lap. She hadn't talked to Mama like that either, like she would have before Mama stopped talking.

If Mama hears, she should hear us laugh.

Polly put her fingers on the green patchwork quilt Mama had finished only a month ago. She traced the embroidered prairie flowers, the delicate needlework patches of sunflowers and grasses that lay sprinkled between other squares of greens, golds, and pale yellows. The prairie flowers Mama had loved so.

"It's so beautiful," said Jessie. "Maybe . . . maybe if Mama gets her mind back . . ." She glanced over at Mama. "*When* Mama gets her mind back, we can help her finish the rose quilt. Wouldn't that be wonderful, Polly? With us helping, it'd get done in no time."

"It would," Polly agreed, and she and Jessie scrambled off the bed and dug in the cedar wardrobe getting out the quilt squares Mama had made for the rose quilt. They spread the patches out on the bed. Beautiful rose colors, deep reds, pinks, and burgundies. Others with intricate needlework designs, thistle and coneflowers, that Mama had made to use on the new quilt. So each of them would have one when they grew up. Mama had told them the quilts were for them.

After filling the lamps and trimming their wicks, Polly and Jessie played with the quilt squares, laughing as their cornhusk dolls tried on the squares as shawls and hid under the green quilt from cowboys, Indians, tornados, and prairie fires.

Sammy jumped up from where he had been sunning himself in the door and scooted outside. They heard a noise, the clatter of a wagon. Polly looked at Jessie. "Did you hear a 'hello'?"

"No," Jessie said, running to the door. They saw Raef Smith. Polly turned and scrambled to close and bar the door. It was too late. The door smashed back open and Raef came in.

"Where's your mama?" he asked, looking the room over.

And then he saw Mama. Polly saw him see her and she looked at Mama too and Mama rocked, and Polly saw Jessie rushing to the rocker and standing beside it, and Mama didn't look up. Just rocked.

"Mrs. Johansson?" Raef Smith said. He stood staring at Mama.

Mama kept rocking, looking straight ahead. Didn't look up. Just rocked.

Raef put his head back, squinted his eyes. "Good Lord," he said, looking back at Polly. She was standing by the door still holding the end of the heavy bolt she had grabbed when they heard him coming.

Polly looked down at the floor. There were sticky clumps of sod all over it from Raef's boots. Jessie had worked so hard on keeping it clean for Mama. The salt. For Mama. And he had sod clumps all over it.

"Papa's home," she said. And she made herself smile. "He's out looking over the fields, seeing what he needs to do first." Polly lied. She had never lied before. Lying was a sin. Like hating.

Raef stared at her. "Your pa?" he said. "Home?"

"Yes, home. He's home." Polly's face felt hot. She wondered if Raef Smith noticed. She just wanted him to think Papa was there. She just wanted him to go.

Raef went to the door, squinted, and looked toward the barley fields. He looked again around the room and Polly noticed his eyes stop on the gun rack above the door. The shotgun wasn't there. Polly had put it in the stable underneath the hayrack. And she had moved the powder horn too. Hidden it and the bag of shot under the manger in the stable. She was glad she had moved them.

Raef walked slowly around the room. He picked up the photograph of Mama and Papa and Elsa and Polly. He ran one finger along the side of the frame and looked at the back. The whole frame was tarnished.

Raef put it back on the sideboard where it toppled to the floor. Jessie ran, stooped and picked it up, putting it back in its place. Raef picked up the quilt pieces and fingered the green quilt.

Jessie stood now between Raef and the door. Polly spoke to her in a low voice. "Get Papa," she said.

Jessie looked blankly back at her, then disappeared out the door. Raef twirled, watching Jessie leave, then turned back to look at Polly. Polly stared at him. She hoped she looked calm. Her heart had not stopped pounding.

Raef turned halfway toward the door again, then shook his head. "Wife told me you took money, girl." He bundled up the quilt pieces inside the quilt. "No one can say I took more'n what should rightfully be mine. You take from me, you make good." He left. Polly ran to the door and clutched the door frame. *Not the quilts.* She opened her mouth to speak but closed it again.

"Your ma would agree," Raef Smith said, looking back at her before getting on the wagon. "She'd agree, girl, she'd want you to make it right." He looked at Polly for a moment and then clucked his teeth to his team.

"Not the quilts," Polly said softly, standing in the doorway, her hands falling from the frame as she stepped out the door and watched Raef riding off. She walked out near the stable and called to Jessie and saw her sister stand up and come out from behind an old haystack and start running toward her.

She hoped the Lord would forgive her for lying. She would ask Him to. Maybe He would. He forgave sinners in the Bible.

9

The Deal

A wind came in the night. It ran across the wild grasses and the new fields and pushed the big bluestem and switchgrass into waves out on the prairie. Polly changed quickly out of her nightgown and went out. The stable stood silent, asleep in the early light. Jessie and Mama were sleeping too.

Polly stood on a slope out from the soddy and the wind tangled her hair, and she watched the same nighthawk she had seen at dusk leave the corncrib for the sky.

A small figure was coming, a horse and rider she thought, but hard to tell and for a moment she thought it might be Papa.

But it was not Papa. It was Raef Smith again.

By the time he was within earshot Jessie had come out and was watching too.

"Hellooo," he called.

Polly pushed her hair off her forehead, squinting in the sun's glare, and watched Raef Smith ride up. She noticed two prairie hens on the side of his saddle. He got off his horse and Jessie stepped back. He stood for a moment, glancing toward the soddy before he said anything.

"The wife and me's been talking. . . . Now we know your pa's not here and your ma, the way she is . . . you'll need some meat."

Polly glanced again at the wild chickens hanging from his saddle. "We're obliged," she said, her heart still pounding. He knew. He knew she had lied. Papa wasn't back.

She sensed there was more. She waited, her heart quickening its beat. Raef went over to the cistern by the side of the house and took a drink, then came back looking out over the fields as he walked. He stopped, looked at the girls again.

"Looks like your pa done most his planting 'fore he left. But you'll be needing more work done. We can turn sod, plow over that old section, over on the north side 'a them new oats." He paused again, looked at the ground and over toward the stable before continuing. "The wife can use some help over at our place." He spit on the ground and continued. "I'll send one of the boys over here one or two days a week. You or your sister, one, can come the same time to work for Ruth. 'Spect the other one'll need to stay here with your ma."

Polly put her hand over her eyes to shield the bright morning sun over Raef's shoulder.

"You understand what I'm saying?" he said.

Polly nodded. She understood. And she *didn't* want to go work for Ruth Smith.

"We'll think of something else come harvesttime. You got hay, feed for your livestock?"

"Yes, sir."

"Might need to take 'em on, temporary, you run out." Raef scratched his chin. "And then again, it could depend on how much work we do over here."

He wanted the animals. That was it. But he could *not* take the animals. Not now or ever.

"Papa'll be back soon. He cut enough marsh hay for the animals before he left."

Raef looked at her. She knew he didn't think Papa would come back but she guessed he couldn't be *sure*. She didn't trust Raef Smith. She didn't know what was fair. But what he said about the animals . . . Gus and Helga and Gerda. . . . She would not part with them. Not ever.

Raef Smith stared at her. And Polly stood there and felt little and alone and afraid to say no. He turned to his horse, looked back at Polly, turned again and handed her the prairie hens. Polly took them and stood squinting at Raef getting on his horse and turning it to go.

"We need our horse and cows, though . . ." Polly said suddenly.

She couldn't see his face. The glare of the rising sun behind him in her eyes. But he was staring at her. She knew that.

"We'll be keeping our horse . . . and cows," she said.

They watched him leave. It looked like rain might be brewing. That was good. The crops could use rain. She would go off and work for the Smiths. But only till Papa came.

They watched the eastern sky darken as Raef rode off.

10

The Workers

*P*olly stood in the wind on the top of the ridge watching the edge of the world for Papa. Maybe the wind was coming from the river valley. Maybe Papa was there loading timber on the wagon now, and he would ride home to them in this wind.

"Come home, Papa," she whispered and Polly stood in the little road on the top of the ridge watching. Waiting. She saw a flock of tiny birds there. Tiny birds swirling in the clouds. She stayed with them a minute and then walked back toward the stable, and the wind threw her bonnet around on her back and she wished she could run to the ridge and look again. But she only turned back for a moment, and kept on walking.

Raef Smith or one of his sons came three times

those first two weeks after Raef told Polly about the deal. They came, mostly turning sod, in fields not tilled since the grasshoppers, and Polly thought they'd try to take over the claim. She had heard Papa say Raef Smith had a land warrant. He might think he could use that to take over their claim, the improvements already made and now him and his sons working the land.

As for now, Polly thought, there was nothing to do. Today she would go and work for the Smiths. Jessie would stay home and do their own chores and take care of Mama.

She looked in the stable. It was still early. The sun came through cracks in the stable walls leaving rose-colored strips on the earthen floor. Jessie had the bridle on Gus. They took him out.

"Will they take Gus and Helga and the calf?" asked Jessie.

"No," Polly said, but she wasn't sure.

"Papa won't like it . . . if we let them take our animals."

"Papa will get them back."

"We should just tell Mr. Smith no."

"We should."

There were no more words. They were afraid.

Afraid to tell Raef no. But afraid or not, Polly thought, she *would* say no. If Raef came for the animals, she *would.*

On her way to the Smiths', Polly's eyes wandered on the prairie, lost in the grasses that dipped into draws and rose quickly again to meet the prairie on the other side. She had heard some people say it was a harsh land, an unforgiving land. Maybe for them that was true. But it would never be for her. For her it was home.

Polly rode on with the wild grasses whispering, whispering in the wind, and the strong old horse swishing through the seed heads. She turned Gus off to the south guiding him down to a place she knew in a gentle valley, into the edge of the great strands of big bluestem that grew there.

Big bluestem, as tall as Gus's shoulders, claiming all the earth it grew on.

Her very home was made from the roots and sod underneath this grass. One-by-two or three-foot slabs of sod, carved out of the land, stacked like giant bricks three feet deep to make the walls of her soddy. Of all the grasses, Polly thought she loved this one best.

Polly turned Gus soon to go on to the Smiths', but her mind stayed on the bluestem.

She saw the Smiths' outbuildings appear over the oats, so she dropped off Gus and left him to graze on the edge of the prairie past the fields. Ruth Smith stood by the clothesline watching her.

"Good morning," Polly said.

"Morning indeed! Halfway to noon."

Ruth Smith told Polly she was not there to play. Polly should be grateful for the work Raef and Paul were doing at her homestead, and Ruth Smith set Polly Johansson to work.

Polly hoed. She carried water to the house. She gathered vegetables. She helped Mrs. Smith boil clothes in the strong lye soap and helped her hang them out in the heavy wind.

Then it was lunchtime. Polly leaned over the boiling water washing dresses and underclothes for Jessie and Mama and herself. Ruth Smith had sent a message to her that she'd be washing, so Polly brought some of their own clothes. It would be easier than spending a day at the river or setting up at home. Ruth Smith looked at the dingy things and told Polly to wash them at lunchtime. So now she shifted between eating the biscuits she brought from home and washing the clothes.

"Your ma still can't talk?"

The voice surprised Polly. She whirled around. Simon!

Before she could answer, Raef and the older boys came out of the soddy along with Ruth Smith, who told Polly to put her things up. Lunch was over.

Polly took the last dress out of the pot and struggled to hang it with the others on the clothesline. It was not easy, for the line was almost too high for Polly to reach. She stood staring at the faded dresses flapping on the line. Faded from so many washings in the same lye soap at home. Papa would bring new calicos and flannels for Mama to make new dresses. She took a quick breath. Mama would be making dresses again. She would. Polly turned and followed Ruth Smith into the soddy.

Inside, Ruth Smith was impatient. She was impatient that she had had to wait for Polly to hang the dress on the line before she could give directions for the afternoon's work. Polly stood by the door, her shoulders stiff, her arms folded tightly. She tried to remember the instructions, her eyes on the floor until the scolding was over. She tried.

And then she sat still in the straight, hard chair where she had begun to sew, her head bent down over the needle and thread. Between her shoulder blades was already beginning to hurt and then she had to churn butter when this was over. She wished she was outside in the wind, but the tedious work had only begun.

The day dragged on with only the promise of more such days of dull work stitching and churning and grinding corn. And never, never pleasing Mrs. Smith. Not that she cared to please Mrs. Smith. She cared only not to be scolded for jobs well done.

Before dusk came Polly rode Gus home, tired and hungry. She found Jessie equally tired and hungry, still in the garden. They looked at the potatoes and frowned. They would need them this winter. They should go ahead and get them out of the ground and store them away in the cellar.

"We could start when we finish with Gus," Polly told her sister.

"I'll rub him down and start digging some out

and you do the dishes. There's not any for supper tonight unless we wash them," Jessie said.

Polly watched Jessie turn Gus toward the stable and she wondered how much time Jessie had spent that day brushing Mama's hair instead of washing dishes. As soon as she thought it, she was sorry. If it helped Jessie feel better to fix Mama's hair then she didn't mind. Not at all. And maybe it helped Mama to feel better. How was she to know?

She turned and went inside. It was cool enough. The light was low but she could see without the lamp. She didn't focus on Mama sitting in the dark by the bed. She poured water into the basin from the pail and put the tin plates in the water, washing them carelessly, quickly putting the dripping plates in the cupboard and turning to scrub the skillet. She frowned at it, then let her eyes scan the familiar walls. They stopped on the photograph on the sideboard. Wiping her hands on her dress, Polly went to the marble top and took down the picture. She held it in her hands looking at it. She looked at her mother in the photograph. The coral comb from Papa in her hair.

"Why'd you leave us, Mama?" she whispered. "Why'd you do it?" Without blinking, Polly looked at Mama in the picture and she did not remember anything except that Mama had left them and now lived in some other place where Polly could not go. And Mama would not listen. Or look. Or talk. And Polly was angry at Mama. And so she lifted her chin and slowly, deliberately, put the picture facedown on the marble.

11

The Night Caller

For three days the girls worked in their garden. The Smiths had not been back. Polly and Jessie finished the supper dishes, then closed the stock in for the night.

Polly sat on the bench outside the door. Jessie came to join her. From inside the soddy they could hear the creak of the rocker as it moved on the uneven earth. And outside, they waited again. Waited for Papa to come home.

They sat on the bench and watched the sun drop low out of the western sky and watched birds swirl up and disappear into tiny dots and watched a low full moon begin to rise. They watched black shadows in the dark green grasses until Polly had to squeeze her eyes shut. And all the time they scanned the horizon for a dot that would be Papa.

And they talked of Papa, remembered Papa.

"First thing! First of all, when he comes, Mama will get better," Jessie said. "He'll make her laugh and laugh."

"Like last winter at the slough. Remember?" Polly smiled. And they talked of how Mama had laughed at Papa skating in his old skates on the frozen slough pond north of the farm.

"I will tell you this Polly, Jessie," he told the girls, "how I won your mama's heart by skating like a racing champion." Papa flew by them swinging his arms and taking low strides. "Always I was the best skater, and the others, they see me coming they give up right away," he had shouted. And then he fell and ended up sitting on the ice in the middle of the pond.

"Best skater in Sweden." Mama had laughed and hugged the two girls to her.

Polly and Jessie smiled remembering.

A stronger breeze started up from the west. Sammy came darting out of the grasses into the house, startling them. They saw little of Sammy these days, especially when the Smiths came to work the land. Jessie went to get cream for his bowl. Polly turned back to the prairie, leaning again on the wall of the soddy, and watched the grasses going on and on.

She bent over and peeped in the soddy. Jessie was stooped beside Sammy at his bowl rubbing his back while he purred and drank his cream. Polly got up and went inside looking back once more at the land. She closed the door. Jessie picked up Sammy and carried him toward Mama and the rocker.

"You better put him down. He's going to scratch you," Polly said.

Jessie put the squirming Sammy on the floor. Polly felt better in the small room tonight, the door latched, the glow of the lamplight and Sammy licking his paws. *He* wasn't afraid. They put on their nightgowns and Polly went to Mama in the chair. She stood there a moment unwilling to say anything.

"Mama? You want to go to bed now?" Polly finally asked. "You want to go to bed? It's time."

And Jessie took Mama's hand. "Come on, Mama, it's all right."

Outside Polly heard the wind and she wondered if Papa would get back before the first frost or even winter, and she knew he'd be back before winter because he'd never leave them there alone in the winter.

The wind moved the door a little . . . and Mama rocked.

"You'll sleep better in the bed, Mama," Polly said.

But it was clear Mama would spend this night in the chair.

So the two girls went to bed, wanting to talk, wanting to hear each other's voice in the dark.

"Remember Papa coming at us on the skates?" Polly whispered, smiling. "Yelling, 'I am Old Man Winter' . . ."

" 'I am Old Man Winter! And I am looking for some trolls!' " Jessie answered, giggling.

Polly said it was time they better get to sleep. She glanced at Mama. Mama sat in the rocker, her head dropped forward. Asleep now. And so the girls lay there and were sleepy and began to drift into that sleep, when Gus neighed. Polly and Jessie heard it at the same time.

Polly got out of bed first, followed by Jessie. They slipped to the window and stared out on the moonlit prairie.

"What is it?" Jessie whispered.

"I don't know."

They watched and saw only the blue black grasses and some dark clouds floating near the moon.

"Something must be out there, or someone . . ." Jessie whispered.

They watched silently. "Over there." Polly pointed to the stable. A dark figure left the stable and came toward the soddy. Jessie held both her hands over her mouth. Polly rushed to the door.

"Quick, Jessie!" She motioned, her hands pointing at the bolt, and bent and lifted it, Jessie at the other end. Jessie's end thudded to the floor. They tried again and awkwardly the bolt inched up and fell at last into the heavy wooden slots. The girls scrambled barefooted back to the small window. The figure was gone. Polly saw a horse tied next to the stable that she hadn't seen the first time. She pointed at it.

"Do you think it's the Smiths?" Jessie whispered.

"I don't know. Probably . . . I don't know." Who else was there out here? Polly thought. But why?

Polly went to the door. Maybe she could see

something through a crack by the frame. She saw little. Just a sliver of moonlit sky.

They waited with only the quiet tick of the clock and the sound of their own breathing and the creak of the door when they leaned too hard against it. A noise by the bed made them turn.

A small clump of sod had fallen from the edge of the ceiling. Polly stared up at the willow rafters. Someone was on the roof. Minutes passed. Polly's eyes searched every corner of the room and darted back to the rafters. And the door moved.

He was outside and trying the door.

Jessie crouched by the wall, her hands over her mouth again, and the knocking came. Three loud knocks.

Clinging close to the wall, Polly edged over beside the window. She gasped. A face was staring in. It was looking straight forward . . . not at her, but toward the corner . . . at Mama. Come to stare at Mama.

Polly backed away and stooped down by the front wall where Jessie crouched. "Simon," she whispered. "It's Simon."

"Why didn't he hello the house?" Jessie whispered back.

"I don't know."

They sat on the dirt floor by the front wall of their soddy. And later they heard the horse again and saw a dark rider on the horse, and they got their blankets and pillows and slept there.

And they dreamed. They dreamed about callers coming in the dark of night. Callers who knocked on doors, came in doors, fell through roofs.

Dreams that woke them. Dreams that sent them again to look out of the window. Just to make sure no one was there.

They were glad Papa had put glass instead of oil paper in the tiny windows because oil paper would be of no use in the middle of the night for checking on callers who wouldn't hello the house.

In the morning they looked outside and saw that everything was in place. The animals, the harnesses, Papa's steel plowshare. Everything. The same as before. There was no sign of a caller coming in the night and taking away their sleep and even their dreams.

12

The Memory

Polly had been on her knees yanking at the stubborn weeds for half the morning and still the job was not done. She sat back and picked mindlessly at the dirt underneath her fingernails and frowned at the bucket she would be hauling water in when she finished weeding. She didn't know Mama was behind her there in the garden, behind the soddy, didn't know when she turned to cool her face in the wind that she would see her mama there looking at her.

"You, what have you done with my babies?"

"Mama?"

"What have you done!"

"I . . . I don't have the babies, Mama. . . ." Polly got to her feet, rubbing her gritty, sunbrowned hands on her dress, and Jessie came running and stood beside her, and Mama shielded her eyes from the sun's glare and peered at them, confused.

"This one," she indicated Jessie with a nod of her head, "will not tell me where they are," Mama said. "Inga. Inga will not tell me . . ."

"It's Jessie, Mama. That's Jessie, remember?"

Polly tried to go to Mama but when she moved, Mama stepped back. Jessie was crying. Polly could hear her choking back her sobs. Polly waited and Mama studied them and Polly wished and wished she would call them by their own names and be their mama again.

Mama's eyes darted away to the fields for a second and back to the girls. "Sven?" Mama said. "He took them?" And Mama turned then from her children and gazed over the barley fields talking to herself. "Sven took them. . . . Does he not know the babies are too little yet? Did I not tell him they are too little?" Mama looked to the open prairie, to where the little bluestem covered the north ridge. "Did he go north? What direction did he go?" she said, looking again at Polly. "You were out here . . . you must have seen . . ."

Polly didn't know what to say. She didn't know what to do. If it was a fever, she'd know.

"Mama . . . Mama, Papa didn't take . . ."

But Mama backed away from Polly. She put her hand up in front, blocking Polly from her sight. And Polly knew Mama was afraid of what Polly had started to say. Mama knew, somewhere inside herself, that Papa did not have the babies.

It had been the wrong thing to say. The truth. Mama had not wanted her to say the truth. Now Polly knew. If this happened again, she would know.

They waited only moments. And then Mama had her hands over her head and over her face and she began to turn around, and Polly thought maybe she would fall and they ran to her.

"Papa's coming soon," Polly said. She took Mama's hand. Jessie ran to hold on to Mama, her arm around Mama's waist. "Did you hear what Polly said, Mama?" Jessie asked and she took Mama's other hand.

They walked to the soddy and led her inside to the rocker. "Papa'll know what to do," Polly said. "When he comes, he'll help you, Mama. And it won't be so long till he gets back." She dusted her hands off on her dress again and got a wet rag. "It won't be so long," she said. She rubbed Mama's forehead with the rag, made the cool rag go over Mama's forehead and onto her hair and after a while Mama's eyes were empty again and Polly's throat was so tight with unshed tears that she could no longer speak.

In a while she would go back to the garden . . . and Jessie would finish grinding corn.

But now she handed Jessie the rag and stood by the small window and remembered the babies that Mama could not remember. Remembered the tiny coat she herself had almost finished. A tiny coat for her first little baby brother. But then Karl had been taken from them. Karl had died. And Polly had ripped out every thread from the tiny coat and she had taken the tiny pieces of carefully cut cloth and tried to bury them out on the cold, frozen land.

Papa had found her there sitting on her heels out on the barren prairie, in the bitter wind, found her sitting there, her nose red, her eyes squeezed shut, gripping the tiny coat. She had tried to make a hole in the earth to put it in but the winter earth was too hard to break open.

Papa had taken out his hunting knife and broken the ground for her and she had buried it. She had leaned into her papa's shoulder and they had walked out farther on the prairie.

And Polly remembered too the winter just past and the second baby.

January and Patrik was born. When Patrik was born, Polly had found something new inside herself. Something that held back. Because Polly was never going to let herself feel what she had felt with Karl. Never. Polly could not make Patrik a coat and indeed there was no time. Only two days. Not enough time even to cut the cloth. But time enough to sit with Mama and rock him and sing to him and let him grasp her finger with his tiny fingers. Time enough to love him same as Karl. And then he was gone too. And Polly did feel what she had felt before. What she had planned on never, never feeling again.

13

The Walker

$\mathcal{P}$olly woke dreaming of rose-colored thistles spreading toward the sunrise. When she was little, her mama had found them growing out on the prairie and had taken her to see them. "Mama," she remembered saying, "they're like the sun." And Mama had smiled.

Polly got up and went to Mama. "I dreamed of the thistles, Mama," she said. "It was a good dream. Remember the thistles, Mama?"

Polly stood waiting and watching her for a minute before turning for the pail to start the milking.

Polly and Jessie went to the creek early that morning, busied with the task of replenishing the household water. They carried buckets to fill one of the empty water casks. They would leave it on the wagon, it would be too heavy to lift.

Gus stood patiently waiting at the stable now after pulling the wagon home. Polly had just taken the harness off the huge horse when something caught her eye. Out on the prairie. Far out near the south ridge. She squinted, and then she saw what it was.

"Jessie," she called. She glanced back and she saw Jessie looking too. At Mama. Walking away. She was a quarter of a mile away, just walking.

Polly watched and walked forward and then began to run out into the tall grasses after Mama.

She heard Jessie behind her calling, "Mama! Mama!" running after her too, and Mama kept on walking, taking no notice of the cries.

Just walking.

Just walking away over the prairie.

The sun seared white in the sky. Polly ran until she had to stop and stoop over to catch her breath. She looked over her shoulder to see Jessie behind her and looked back again to see Mama still walking.

"Jessie! Go get Gus! Go back and get him!" she shouted. Jessie stopped and stared at Polly, bewildered.

"What?" she said. "What?"

"Get Gus. Now!"

Jessie looked at Mama and back at Polly and Polly could tell Jessie didn't want to go back. Jessie wanted to follow Mama. Jessie wanted to get Mama and make her come back.

"I'll go after Mama! You get Gus and come back! We need Gus!" cried Polly, looking back and forth between her little sister and her mother.

"Go!" she yelled. And then Polly ran again after Mama, and Jessie ran back toward the house and Gus.

Polly stumbled, picked herself up, ran and ran until she caught Mama. She could hardly breathe. "Mama," Polly choked out, grabbing on to Mama's arm. "Stop!"

Mama did not stop. So Polly clung to Mama's arms with both her hands, half leaning on Mama, and walked along with her until she had breath to talk. But when there was breath to speak, there was nothing to say. Mama pushed at Polly's hands to loosen them from her arm and when Polly would not let go, Mama walked on, toward the west, dragging Polly with her. Polly tried to pull. She tried not to let Mama go but Mama pulled too, gently but a strong pull, a slow deliberate pull, and Polly could not stop her.

"Mama! Please no!" Polly screamed as Mama pulled her arm away from Polly's grasp. But she followed again, and pulled again, and walked on with Mama because there was nothing else to do.

A thought came to her. She could not keep walking. They might not be able to find their way back if they kept on. There was no rhyme or reason to the path Mama was taking. Polly's eyes scanned toward the soddy. It had been out of sight awhile hidden behind the swells of the land. They were still on high ground. Polly turned searching for Jessie. She did not see her.

There was a place she thought might be the river north of the homestead. Tall slough grasses followed the river's edge there. But she couldn't be sure. There was nothing else but grass and sky. Nothing to see but vast tablelands and low rolling hills, grass, and sky. Cloud shadows deepened their colors for fleeting moments, but everything looked the same and the shining prairie reached out on and on.

Polly checked the sun and its position and looked at her shadow. She could always go north and find the river and follow it home. *She* could get home. But could Jessie find them? Jessie's sense of direction had never been good. Even on Gus, Jessie could get lost looking for her and Mama now.

Polly's heart fell. What if Jessie was off course just a little and didn't see them, for the land rolled and dipped. And Jessie might just keep going . . . looking . . . too far. Or what if Jessie veered off toward the slough grasses up river and got lost. Papa said to stay out of the wet meadows up there. Overrun with the tallest of the slough grasses, the slough there was dense, and spread out a mile or so from the river. Polly had been running and now walking with Mama for a mile, maybe two already.

"Jessie's coming for us on Gus, Mama! I sent her back for Gus. She can't find us if we keep walking! She could get lost, Mama!"

Polly stopped. "Mama, stop! I can't go on."

But Mama looked straight through Polly, and Polly knew Mama didn't hear her. Polly knew. And Mama walked away. She walked away and Polly stood there and watched her mother walk away from her into the prairie. Polly gasped and started to sob silently because she knew there was nothing, nothing in the world she could do but let her go.

She watched Mama go until she was out of sight,

swallowed up by the grasses and prairie flowers that they had always loved. She stood there then just looking and she started thinking she hated the prairie grasses and she started running toward where Mama had disappeared, but she remembered Jessie on Gus and now maybe the grasses would swallow Jessie too and so she stopped and turned back and walked in the direction of home. Just walked. Just walked like Mama. After a time she saw a speck coming and it was Jessie on Gus.

14

The Lookers

*A*fterwards, they had gone home.

After Mama walked away.

After Jessie came and ran from the horse to the top of the ridge looking everywhere. After they rode Gus to the top of other ridges to look.

After Jessie's screams . . .

They had gone home, silently on the horse's wide back. He gently plodded home. Polly let him have his head and Gus took them back home. They would not tell the Smiths now. If they told the Smiths, they'd take them away. And Mama would come back, like she did before, and they wouldn't be there. Polly promised Jessie they'd go look for Mama and for days they rode out on the prairie into the sea of grass. Looking.

It had been ten days. . . .

Polly was standing on the rise behind the soddy. She was standing by the two small crosses there. She remembered both buryings. Jessie's tears. Mama's sobs. The aching in her own throat and eyes. She had stood by Papa with her chin high as he read from the Bible. She had blinked back every tear. Like Papa. She had loved the babies so much.

Now her eyes wandered over the grasses that covered the graves and went on and on to the ridge and beyond.

Forever. It seemed.

All the grasses of the prairie, switchgrass, big bluestem, Indian grass. Papa had taught her many of their names. She was standing in a patch of porcupine grass now. She was touching its long ribbonlike leaf. It loosely curled and hung, tossing in the wind, blowing sideways off the stem. It was beautiful. . . .

She was thinking about Mama and about Jessie. And she thought she would just let Jessie think that she could have made Mama come back. She would let Jessie blame her for Mama being gone.

Why shouldn't she?

She blamed herself.

❦

Polly left the rise and went to the stable to milk Helga. She found Jessie was already there and was finishing up. Polly didn't realize how long she had been out back.

"After we strain this and after breakfast, let's go out and look again. Right after breakfast," Jessie said, carrying the heavy pail with both hands to the stable door.

Polly wasn't listening. She was looking at Jessie's long braid down her back. It looked like she had combed it with her fingers. And slept in it. Polly's fingers went to her own hair. Her two long braids were the same way. She pushed a loose strand behind her ear.

"Right after breakfast?" Jessie said again. "Let's go look then."

"We have to start working the garden again, Jessie. That's our food. We don't know when Papa'll be back."

"I'm going after breakfast. You don't have to

come." Jessie left the stable carrying the pail.

"The lima beans'll be ripe before this week's over. You saw all those weeds."

"They'll be all right."

"They will not. You want Papa to come back and see those weeds've taken over? You want everything overrun with weeds and ruined when Papa comes?!"

"Papa would want us to keep looking," Jessie said, her voice loud. "And I'm going."

"No, Jessie," Polly repeated, "Mama's gone."

"You can't stop me."

"I can and I will."

"You cannot. How are you going to stop me?" Jessie challenged.

Polly said nothing. She took the milk and got ready to strain it. She was trying to say the things she thought Papa would want her to say. After all, it was up to her, she *was* the oldest. It had been too long. Ten days. The tops of the onions were yellow and falling over. It would be good to go ahead and get them out of the ground. And the weeds. . . . They *needed* to work the garden.

"How?" Jessie continued. "How are you going to stop me?" she said accusingly.

Polly wanted to scream at Jessie. She was trying to act grown up . . . like Elsa would have . . . but Jessie wouldn't let her. Well, she wasn't a grown-up. And she was tired of trying to act like one. And the garden could go to rot. Let it. Then they wouldn't have any vegetables to eat. If that's what Jessie wanted. She sure wasn't going to fight her every step of the way.

But she didn't say that.

If she said it then Jessie might realize she was right and maybe they wouldn't go look, and she didn't really want to stop looking, did she? She didn't want to . . . not really. It could be Mama was still alive, she told herself. She could have been found by a soldier maybe . . . or by the Sioux, although Polly knew there weren't any Sioux hunting there anymore. Papa had told her. But maybe . . .

So every day they continued to ride out on the prairie looking for their mother who had walked away. And every day the garden suffered from neglect, though they spent what time they had left over tending it when they weren't looking for Mama.

15

The Orphans

*J*essie had been quiet for days. She didn't want to go look for Mama anymore. She didn't ask accusing questions anymore. She didn't blame Polly anymore. Jessie had given up.

Ruth Smith sent for Polly just once a week now, and when Ruth Smith asked, Polly said, "Mama's still not right." But Polly did not say Mama was gone.

For three weeks they had searched.

It had been too long.

The sun was hardly over the horizon, the wind was blowing, and all at once Polly felt like running. She ran out past the cornfield, past the oats, and on out onto the open prairie where she finally stopped out of breath and she almost laughed. Because it had been so long since she had played. So long since she had run in the wind. She looked out over the grasses to the sky, to the muted shadowy blues at the prairie's ends. And Polly knew that if she ever did get to those ends, that if she flew there like the eagles, she would find the tall grasses again. The sloping hills and tablelands, meadows, sloughs. All covered with the prairie grasses she loved.

She stood breathing hard and there she saw the dragonfly. It quivered there in the midst of the tall bluestem, its wings transparent and dabbed with blue and black along the edges, and Polly knew if she moved it would go. "Look, Mama," she remembered telling her mother when she was little. "See its wings!" She had wanted Mama to see the dragonfly through her eyes and make it beautiful for Mama.

And then the dragonfly was gone. It swept across the grasses into the prairie and was gone. When Polly squinted she thought she could see the same blue in the grasses.

And she stood there and it came to her that she could no more have stopped her mama from sweeping away into this prairie than she could have stopped the dragonfly. No one was to blame. But

Polly wished she could go home and find Mama still there. "Look, Mama," she would say. "Look at the prairie," and then the prairie world would be beautiful for her mother too.

❦

Polly pushed open the damper after poking at the corn bread. It was still wet inside. Jessie rushed in with the milk bucket, spilling some as she put it on the table in her hurry. "Simon's coming," Jessie said. She was out of breath. Sammy, apparently sensing the stranger, ran out of the door, not even the prospect of the spilled milk enticing him to stay, and Jessie moved into the dark corner beside the bed watching Polly and the door.

"Your mama talking?" Simon asked, appearing suddenly in the doorway. Almost as if he knew.

Polly tugged at a strand of hair that fell loose by her face and pressed both her lips together tightly. She didn't answer. She saw him look sideways at Jessie in the corner and saw his eyes searching the room. Polly looked straight at him, the strand of hair falling back over her eye. She pushed it away and twisted it into her braid with her fingers.

"She's gone. She just took off walking more'n two weeks ago. We tried to stop her, but it wasn't any use."

It was out of her mouth before she hardly knew she had said it. She should *not* have said it.

Simon stared at Polly speechless. Then he shook his head. "Land's sakes!" he said finally. He stared at Jessie again and left as suddenly as he had appeared.

Polly sat on the bed. What had she done?

❦❦❦

The next morning Ruth Smith came herself. She appeared suddenly at the door, startling them. Jessie, holding a dripping dishcloth, took a step backwards almost tripping on the stool, and Polly's chest tightened.

Ruth Smith whisked in the door after a brief look around the room. She wasted no time.

"Raef and I've been talking. It falls to us to look after your well being. You're orphans now." Jessie looked at Polly, confused. Polly slowly shook her head.

Orphans! We're not orphans! she thought.

"Raef leaves for Fort Hartsuff the end of the week. They may know some folks that can take you in over that way . . . that can take you down to Kearney if need be. But the best we can figure is the orphan trains. Somebody there's bound to know how to get you on one of those trains."

Jessie's face drained. Polly glanced at Jessie and glared back at Ruth Smith.

Ruth Smith fidgeted with her collar, pulling it away from her neck as though it was too hot. "You'll need to pack a bag with all your clothes and anything else you want to keep," she told them. "Why don't you do that now?" she urged. "Go on. Go ahead."

"But we are *not* orphans," Polly said.

"I know it's hard for you to see, but . . ." Ruth Smith studied Polly as she spoke. "Your pa, he's been gone and now your ma . . ." She stopped completely for a moment, then began again. "We can't take on two more. We feel for you bein' alone now but it's the only thing. It won't be as bad as you think."

Polly's legs felt weak. It *would* be as bad as she thought! It would.

Those trains took children away into the plains

and prairies, stopping in little towns where people would sometimes be waiting to take the orphans as their own. Polly had heard of those trains. And to Polly, the stories of those trains had always seemed like the troll tales Papa told them from the old country. And so when Ruth Smith spoke of them, at first, they did not seem real.

Polly grabbed Jessie's hand and stared at Mrs. Smith.

"Well, don't look like that. I don't know what else you expect us to do. Have your things ready Friday. Raef'll be by for you then."

They stood in the doorway and watched her leave. The horse tossed its head. They heard its soft nicker, heard the heavy creaking of the wagon as it lurched forward and slowly moved away. Day after tomorrow Raef Smith would come for them. They went out and stood in the bright sun and watched until she was nothing but a small spot near the horizon, and a silence lingered.

"We're not orphans," Polly said.

16

The Trader

The next morning they sat on an old quilt in front of the soddy shelling lima beans. Tomorrow they would go with Raef Smith. Unless they could come up with something. The minutes flew by. The beans popped into the bowl. And Polly did not know what to do.

"Somebody's comin'," Jessie said, pointing.

They stood up, waiting, squinting in the bright yellow sun, watching the small dark thing that moved slowly on the rim of the south ridge. *If only . . .*

But it was a single wagon, closed in. And a single horse. Not a pair, like Papa's young team.

It's not Papa, Polly thought.

Maybe it was someone who could help. They

had talked about it. About what to do if someone came. About who to trust.

They asked themselves the questions again and again but no more had the answers than when they had first questioned themselves. Probably no one would come anyway.

Their eyes followed the traveler, their faces motionless. They watched.

"Maybe a circuit rider," Polly said.

They heard him when he was still a half mile off. "Hellooo the house!"

It was a peddler. He was old and he was dirty, his beard permanently stained with coffee. He motioned to the side of his wagon, a peeling indication of what was once a wares sign.

"Have you been by the Smiths'?" Polly asked.

"Been by there."

Polly stared at him. It was the wrong answer.

"Said there was a claim this way . . ." He started to say more, but stopped short. "Them folks said they was lookin' out for you."

No. Polly shook her head. No.

"Is that all they said?" Her breath was short. She stumbled over the words. She wanted to know. "Did they tell you about our mother?"

"Said your ma went loco."

Polly stared. Stared at him and wondered why the words should overwhelm her so.

"They're not looking out for us!"

The peddler wasn't listening. He scraped at the edge of his boot with some sort of file.

"Let us go with you to Hartsuff!" Polly said. Her papa would have to come by there on his way back.

"I don't take no passengers."

"Just to Fort Hartsuff. We can bring food. We're not any trouble."

"Told you once. Don't take no passengers. You got them folks. They's watching out for you."

Polly stared at the peddler. He sounded so sure. He didn't understand. Why wouldn't he help them? Someone should help them. They were children. But she looked hard at the old man and she knew he wasn't going to help.

It was all right anyway. It was. They could miss Papa at the fort and what if he got here, and they were gone? At least she didn't have to wonder what would happen if they did leave.

"We'd like to see your goods," Polly said slowly. Somewhere inside herself she didn't want him to leave just yet.

The peddler got down and opened up the back of his wagon. He took out a long pole to secure the lid he lifted. She looked in the wagon. There were kettles and skillets, sacks of flour, small bags of salt, and a box of tea. A small compass. Wool. Linen.

Suddenly her eyes came back to the compass.

Lying there among his goods, a small brass compass, shining in the sun.

In that instant, she knew what to do.

Polly picked it up. "How much?" she asked, frowning.

Too much, she was told.

Slowly she put it down, her heart galloping, and picked up a bag of coffee, put it back. Her fingers reached and touched a skillet. But her eyes stayed on the compass.

"Can we trade? For the compass? We have a silver frame. Sterling. It's real pretty," Polly said, looking at the peddler.

"I'll look at it. Maybe. Depends," he said.

And he did trade and the brass compass was theirs and Polly held it in her hand.

When the peddler had left, she told Jessie.

"We will go into the prairie," she said.

17

The Hiders

The summer days were turning cruel, hotter than Polly remembered. As soon as the peddler left, Polly got two canvas bags. She and Jessie gathered together as many sunflower seeds, turnips, carrots, dried squash, potatoes, and preserves as they could stuff into the small bags. Polly stopped and glanced around the room.

Jessie grabbed the quarter round of cheese and a tin of jerky, anxious to leave quickly. Polly got two blankets, a tarpaulin, and some small willow poles, and they were ready.

That afternoon they rode Gus deep into the prairie through the big bluestem and then the tall slough grass that grew near the river. Upstream they came to the big slough. They crossed the river there to the north side, found a deer path, and followed it several hundred feet into the tall grasses. Frightened shrews and meadow mice scurried out of their way.

They took the supplies and with the compass moved farther away from the deer path into the slough grasses pushing through grass tangled with peavines and wild tubers, chose a place to leave their supplies, and before dusk Gus carried them back to the soddy.

There at home, Polly put a new collar on Sammy's neck. She made it from a scrap of heavy cotton drill and it carried an embroidered message. N. RIVER GRASS, it said. Sammy would carry their message to Papa when he came home.

And so after carrying their things into the grasses to make a camp, and letting loose their animals at home, the children walked away into the prairie they hoped would save them and hide them and keep them till Papa came.

It was different leaving the homestead on foot, looking back at the soddy that sat so still and alone now.

Near dusk, the colors of the prairie darkened. Polly and Jessie walked north and then west following the braided river north of Papa's claim until they came to the place where the wet meadows spread out almost a mile or more. Willows on river sandbars cast long shadows. And the far hills darkened with the oncoming night.

They waded across. A twisted log marked the deer path and turned the children into the slough. They'd heard the stories. Animals drowned in sloughs near Fort Dodge in Iowa. Indians trapped in prairie fires in giant sloughs along the bigger rivers. But they would not lose their bearings. They had the compass.

Night was almost upon them when they reached the camp, the land low and surrounded by the tall slough grass. Sheet lightning flashed in the southern sky, only flickers in the dark grasses. The dense cordgrass and sedges had been flattened there by deer or bison. Polly and Jessie managed a small lean-to with their tarp and the poles, and ate tomatoes in the dark for supper. Wet, tasty tomatoes that were messy and left them wanting more.

They got the blankets and lay down and wished they had brought their pillows. Excited and nervous, they fell asleep anyway but were awakened by thunder cracking everywhere, making horrible popping noises over their heads. Polly sat on her blanket at the edge of the lean-to, her arms hugging her knees, her eyes searching the tossing grasses above them and seeing only the flickering sky. She waited, and later rain splattered onto her face and began to drip off the edges of the canvas, so she crawled into the lean-to with Jessie and they crouched as far back as they could get and Polly wished they were in the soddy with its walls and leaking roof, and wished they were safe.

The storm passed quickly, and Polly and Jessie were left in the unfamiliar camp. They listened to rabbits and rats skittering through the grass, and what they thought might be a deer.

Before light they were awake again, waiting. The night had been tiresome. They had blisters from the long walk in Papa's old bullhide boots they'd worn as protection from rattlers out on the upland prairie. But Polly insisted they keep them on. The winds that covered the prairies didn't reach deep into the grasses where Polly and Jessie waited that first day, so they were hot and they rationed their food and drank extra water to make the hollow feelings in their middles ease. But Polly was glad to be hiding in the sea of grass. Surely the Smiths would not bother to search for them in a sea of grass.

The second day. They felt the heat even more. They had cuts on their hands, their faces, from the leaves of the cordgrass, serrated and tough. Polly frowned at her hands, the cuts now swollen and red, sore. Dirty. She scratched on fresh mosquito bites. She hated these mosquitoes. And the flies too. Polly frowned at standing water nearby. Not fresh. Maybe even with mosquito eggs in it. "Listen," she said, "let's follow the deer trail back to the river. We can hide there in the grass, just for a spell. We can drink more there, and we can refill the canteen." Jessie stood, eager to start.

The river wandered over the sand and cooled their blisters. Their eyes darted downriver. One of the Smith sons could be out combing the riverbed looking for them. They didn't stay long. They brushed their footprints away and scrambled back to wait on an old willow log. Hidden.

Mid-afternoon Jessie thought she saw a rattler.

It slithered quickly through the rushes and by the time she called out for Polly to look, it was gone.

"We've never seen a rattler in the slough. It must've been some other snake," Polly told Jessie.

Yet they were still and quiet and afraid.

"No matter," Polly said. "We're going to see more before this is over. More snakes. It's no different than the ones we've seen on the homestead."

"Yes, no different," Jessie echoed, but they were only words to Jessie.

They drank more water. The quiet rush of the wind rippled through the tops of the grasses over their heads, and now and then Polly told stories to pass the time, stories Mama and Papa used to tell them and stories about what they'd do when Papa came home.

The day dragged on and that night, back at their camp the mosquitoes came. In swarms. They moved through the tall grasses from out of the wet meadows where they lived. First only in numbers the children were used to. Then more than they could imagine. Polly and Jessie tried to get under the tarpaulin. It didn't work. It was near dark and too late to go back to the river. So they scrunched in their blankets with their hands over their faces and waited. Waited while the mosquitoes covered their hands, biting, sucking the blood. Waited until the mosquitoes left.

❦

For four nights and three days, they waited. In the dark and in the wind and rain, under shadowy moons and scorching suns in a sea of grass that went on forever.

In all those days, even though Polly wished and hoped and prayed for Papa to come, in all those times, she felt a part of the land and loved the dark and the rain and the sun and the winds and the grasses because they hid them from a world that could take them away forever.

18

The Believer

$\mathcal{P}$olly began to think that perhaps her plan would work until Simon came that day. The slough had dried out since midsummer, their supplies were lasting, the slough grasses were tall and thick from fires and spring and summer rains. But for Jessie the chance of becoming lost in the slough still loomed. And there was little Polly could say to completely take away Jessie's fears.

Jessie was holding the compass that day. The brass shining in her palm, the needle pointing north and south. Always north and south. Always steady. Comforted by Polly's promises that they could not get lost with the compass, they could afford to wait for Papa, she cradled it that day in her hand, watching, and then the shouts came.

"Your ma's back . . ." It was a distant call at first but Polly and Jessie heard the words, faint but clear. And it was Simon's voice, Polly was almost sure.

At first Jessie just stared at Polly, her eyes suddenly bright and eager and Polly felt something deep within herself, something like hope.

"She's come back! Mama's come back! Did you hear?" Jessie began, her face shining. She stood up and laughed. "Did you hear?"

Polly stood too and grabbed Jessie's shoulders and whispered to wait. Something told her to wait. It was not Papa. It was Simon. "Wait," she whispered again. "It could be a trick, Jessie."

But Jessie was clapping her hands, her face ablaze, her breath quick. Polly knew Simon would never see her deep in the grasses, but he could hear her, he could find them. If she wasn't quiet, he could *find* them.

Polly pulled Jessie down. "Don't say anything, Jessie," she whispered.

"But Mama's back," Jessie said.

Polly put her hand over Jessie's mouth. "Stop it! Stop talking!" she breathed. It wasn't true. Mama would not have come back. For minutes she held her hand over Jessie's mouth. Jessie's eyes, brimming with giant tears, searched Polly's face.

"Come on out, you little fools! You want to die out here?"

Polly shushed Jessie again. "Don't," Polly whispered. "Listen to me."

Jessie pushed Polly's hand away, her face flushed from the excitement of Simon's message and her anger at Polly.

"Mama's back," Jessie insisted, clamoring to stand again. Polly once again pulled her down.

"We'll go, but later. Don't you see? It could be a trick. It's Simon."

Jessie was furious but for now she glared silently at Polly.

"When he leaves, after he leaves, we can go to the soddy. And see for ourselves. We can find out if it's true. Don't you see? We don't have to go with him."

Simon's voice called again over the grass. "Your ma, she sure wants to see you two!"

More promises.

"He's leaving," Jessie whimpered, huge tears spilling out of her eyes, as Simon's voice began to fade.

"It's all right. We'll go see by ourselves, Jessie! We'll go see ourselves . . ."

"She must've been staying with someone. . . . And now she's come for us . . . and . . ." Jessie stopped. "You don't believe him . . . do you, Polly? You don't believe Mama's back."

"You know how long we searched," Polly whispered. "You know . . . how long."

"She *is* back! Let's go *now.* What if Mama leaves, Polly? What if she won't wait on us to get there when Simon says he can't find us."

"She'd wait. She'd know he has to search all over. We'll go tomorrow . . . soon as the sun's up."

They heard Simon's voice calling again, blurring in the distance down the river farther away. "Your ma's back! She wants to see you two . . ."

Jessie's eyes were huge, staring in the direction of the fading voice. She rocked gently back and forth, her hands to her mouth, and her breathing became hard. Polly put her arm around Jessie and squeezed her close, her own eyes watching the tangle of grasses before them.

They sat and waited and listened. Now Simon's calls were somewhere way above them. Somewhere above the grasses spreading over the wide prairie like the wind. Tiny and soft and far away. Some-where else.

They sat and waited and listened as Simon's voice got harder and harder to hear.

Suddenly Jessie screamed. "No!" She stumbled to her feet and began tearing through the tall grass. "Wait!" she screamed after Simon. "Wait!" She stumbled and got to her feet and charged after the voice that promised her Mama was back.

Somehow when Jessie fled, Polly suddenly felt afraid of the grass, though it all happened so fast and Polly had no time to think, but seeing Jessie swallowed up so quickly by the grass, she felt afraid.

She grabbed for the canteen. And for the com-pass . . .

It wasn't there.

She couldn't find it. "Jessie!" she called, look-ing over her shoulder and then back to the canvas, the blankets, and then she remembered, she re-membered, Jessie had the compass. Jessie was hold-ing it. She had it when she left. So Polly ran after Jessie into the grass, tried to run, tripped, picked herself up, fought her way through the thick grasses and vines. It was impossible to *really* run. But she could hear Jessie's screams for Simon and followed the screams and found Jessie gasping, sitting on the ground, tears covering her face.

Polly listened for Simon, but all she heard was something so faint and far away she didn't even know if it was real.

And then Polly screamed.

"Siiii . . . monnnn!"

She didn't think. She just screamed Simon's name as loud as she could. Jessie stopped crying and stared at Polly and they both listened and all they heard was the rushing of the breeze somewhere up in the grass and the clear sounds of meadowlarks some distance away and nothing of Simon who came calling about their mama.

For a long time they sat there, sat on the spongy ground and listened and called again and listened to the wind whispering above them and watched it tumbling the tops of the grasses over their heads.

Jessie got up on her knees looking at Polly. "I want to go see Mama now."

Polly breathed deeply. The heat was stifling and she pushed her sweat-drenched bangs off her forehead. "All right," Polly agreed. They would go now and let Jessie see if it was true, see if Mama had come back. She wiped her face again, and the sticky dampness under her braids next to her neck, and turned for her little sister and the compass. They would go to the river, south to the river and follow it to the land they knew.

"Give me the compass."

Jessie sank back to the earth fingering the pocket in her dress, her face turning ashen.

"Jessie!" Polly cried. "You've got the compass, Jessie!"

Polly stooped beside Jessie, whose panicked eyes searched Polly's, tears brimming over but no words.

"Jessie, where is it? You had it!" Polly cried. Jessie's sobs began.

"Where was it? In your pocket?"

"In my hand," Jessie managed.

"Then where is it?" Polly's eyes desperately combed the ground. "Stop crying and help me look. You must've dropped it here somewhere." Polly scrambled about on her hands and knees. She looked back. "Help me!" she cried.

But Jessie sat staring ahead, staring into the dense boundless green of the grasses, the bronzed yellows and greens blurring before her.

Polly bit her lip and crept into the surrounding

bunches of stems and blades, her hands exploring the dirt underneath, her eyes probing behind each cluster of stems.

"I fell down," Jessie said. "I dropped it then."

"Fell down? Fell down where? Here?"

"Back there." Jessie indicated the grasses behind her.

"You dropped it and you left it?!" Polly cried.

"I . . . I . . . don't know. Maybe . . ." Jessie sobbed. "I didn't want him to leave without us."

The words hung still in the air.

Without the compass they were lost.

19

The Searcher

Polly's eyes followed a beetle crawling slowly up a weed deep among the shadowy cordgrass. She sat in the damp, still heat of the slough and she swallowed and her mouth was dry and sticky. Their dresses were dirty and wet from crawling and sitting.

"All right," she said slowly. "Let's see if we can find our way back to our things." She pushed herself to her feet, her hands sinking into the spongy ground. Her eyes moved up and down the grass and rushes. "Maybe we'll see stalks we broke getting here. Maybe we'll see the place you fell."

Jessie looked up at Polly, her tears drying on her face.

"Maybe we can find the compass."

Jessie looked at the bulrushes and thick grasses

around her. A cattail bobbed up and down. "What if we can't?"

Polly didn't answer.

Jessie got up and followed Polly silently. Their hands pushed through the looming grasses and rushes.

They walked on freshly opened blisters, and hardly noticed the stinging pain. Over and over toothed edges of cordgrass sliced at their hands, leaving small wet beads of blood. But they kept on, pushing through the grass, opening the way.

They looked for footprints in the muck. They looked for stalks, broken when Jessie ran. Or fell. But the tough tangle of stalks everywhere, all so close together, told them nothing.

Polly stopped and Jessie moved up beside her. "What?" Jessie wanted to know.

Polly shook her head. "The compass isn't here," she said. "There's nothing here, nothing to show us the way back. We just need to try to get out of here. . . . If we could get to the river, we could find the deer path."

"Which way's the river?" Jessie asked. She looked around, confused.

"I don't know." Polly stared up at the sky. She

could hardly see the sun, and the puzzle of shadows gave no clue. "There's no telling."

They stood there. The quiet rush of the wind rippled through the tops of the grasses over their heads. Polly listened. She didn't think they'd be able to hear the river. The river was quiet and the dense grasses would block its sound unless they were close. She listened for anything that might give some clue.

Polly could see nothing but grass in front of her. But when she stood on her tiptoes and tilted her head up, she could see far hills and ridges. She squinted at them, studying them. She didn't know them.

"We'll just walk in a straight line, toward one hill," Polly decided. "Maybe we'll get to the river."

"What if we don't?" Jessie asked. "What if we don't and we can't find our way out?"

"We'll either get to the river or wind up on the other side of the slough. *Out* of the slough, Jessie, don't you see?"

They walked.

And from time to time Polly would see the far

ridges and hills. When the grass was not in the way, when she was not covering her eyes to keep serrated leaves from cutting at her face, her eyes. When she was not moving around impenetrable cordgrass, or around water knee-deep, full of cattails and bulrushes and too wide to cross. When she was not looking for footprints and seeing only dense roots.

So when she looked again, the hills were changed. And she would start again. Trying to walk in the direction of just one hill. They walked. And they watched low clouds gather over the slough and Jessie thought Polly would find the way back.

They wandered on and on and a new fear grew. They could be circling. Or they could be going parallel to the river. Polly did not know how long they had been walking. It was hard to breathe. She was afraid. But she could not stop now. So she kept on walking. Beyond her, beyond the slough, lay the upland prairies, the switchgrass, the Indian grass. The big bluestem.

Suddenly a covey of birds burst up, their wings pushing on air, brushing on grass, out and up into the sky. Surprised, the girls stopped. They were tired and hot. And they were lost. A sinking feeling came in the pit of Polly's stomach.

"Maybe we'd be better off staying put so if anyone comes along the river we could hear them," Polly said. "And then we'd know which way the river is, which way to go to get there."

She looked over at Jessie. "You stay here. I'm going to look for the way out. I'm going by myself and will call to you as I go, Jessie. You stay. Then I can get back. I'll stay close enough to hear you."

Jessie didn't want to stay by herself.

"If we both go, then we can't get back here. Don't you see? We want to hear Simon if he comes back by. So we can go in the right direction to get to the river ourselves."

"I don't care," Jessie cried. "I don't want to stay here alone." Her eyes were wild and she put her arms around herself and began to tremble. Her nerves. All her life, if Jessie felt bad she'd get nervous and start shaking. Polly had no patience for it now. The heat of the day was already upon them and an anger was rising in Polly.

"Stop it, Jessie!" Polly shouted. "We're in enough trouble without you starting that! I'm try-

ing to get us out of here. We are *lost! Lost,* Jessie!"
Suddenly Polly's eyes filled with tears and she
stopped yelling. How could Jessie have been so fool-
ish, so careless? The compass . . . she wanted the
compass back. She wiped the falling tears off her
cheeks with the backs of her hands and glared at
Jessie. "Now, you keep calling to me and I'll call
back."

Polly tramped off into the dense growth, anger
replacing her fear. She scratched on sore mosquito
bites. She hated the mosquitoes. She hated the flies.
Surely she *could* find her way out. The compass was
gone but she was *going* to find her way out of here.
Maybe she was close.

"Jeee . . . sssieeee . . ." she called.

"Pooo . . . llyyyy . . .!" Jessie was frightened.
Polly could tell. And her voice was hoarse too from
the yelling earlier when she ran off.

The ground became soggy, and Polly came upon
a small place with standing water. She had been
moving slowly, careful not to cut her hands again on
the grass and she pushed aside the grass and saw a
heron, a great blue heron slowly taking wing.
It lifted up toward the light and the greens in
the grasses reflected on its feathers. It must have

heard her coming and yet sensed no danger. The small ripples it left behind in the standing water dispersed.

"Jeee . . . ssieeee . . ." Polly started trying to stomp down some of the grass, to make a little path. The ground was soggy there. "Jeee . . . ssie! There's a place over here with some water," Polly called.

Maybe it meant the river was nearby. She kept on trying to push down the grass. She was in a gully, a depression. If she could just make a little path to drier ground, higher ground, maybe she'd see the river right around here!

Suddenly she realized. Jessie hadn't called back.

Polly stopped, her heart stopped. "Jeee . . . ssieee!"

And then faintly she heard her sister. "Poo . . . lyyy . . ."

Polly moved toward the voice, until she heard Jessie clearer.

"Jee . . . ssie! Come over here! Can you hear me? There's water over here!" Polly kept calling. All the time calling.

And she did not stop, she did not stop. Jessie had to hear her.

And Jessie came.

Polly wouldn't go so far away now.

In the nearby grasses, in earshot of Jessie, Polly walked back and forth, trying to cover different areas. But it was all the same. More cordgrass, more bulrushes, more vines.

The sun was still hidden behind the low hanging clouds. She could not find their camp or supplies or the river. She could not find the compass. She could not find the way out.

❦❦❦

Finally she went back and dropped to her knees on the squishy ground, exhausted. She sat back resting on her heels.

"When are we going to drink some of the water?" Jessie asked.

Polly frowned. Dinner so long ago, before all this, had been only a dried pumpkin ring and left them hungry. But they didn't really care. It didn't matter. They just wanted water. They just wanted to do something about the thirst. "Two swallows," Polly said, "that's all. Just two."

"But we've found this," Jessie said, looking at the little pool of water around the rushes.

"Yes, but it won't be good like river water. It's not fresh. It may have bug eggs in it or something. We don't have to use it yet."

Jessie frowned at the little area of water. "You think it'd make us sick?"

"It might."

They drank silently from the canteen. It was not enough.

Polly glanced at Jessie. She was still trembling, but she was not complaining and Polly regretted her earlier anger. It had been *her* idea to hide in the slough in the first place. She couldn't keep on blaming Jessie.

"We'll sit still awhile. Maybe it'd help this thirst. We won't sweat as much if we're still. And we won't need as much water. Don't you think?" Polly said.

"I don't know," Jessie whimpered, almost crying.

"It seems that way to me. That's what we're going to do," Polly continued. "Then we'll find our way out of here. I know . . . you plait my hair tighter, tight but real neat so it doesn't pull, and I'll do yours. It'll be cooler. It'll keep it off our necks."

So they waited there on the wet ground, and Polly said it was all right because she knew she could find her way out of the slough. They waited until the light faded, until the heat's power lessened and then Polly walked away in the slough again.

"Poooo . . . llyyyy . . ."

"Jeeee . . . ssieeee . . ."

"Poo . . . llyyyy . . ." Back and forth, the names drifted through the slough holding them together.

Polly frowned at her hands, scabs swelling on the cuts. They hurt. It was not going to work. It was too hard, too tiring struggling through the slough, forcing her way around the tangled clusters of huge grass stalks, hungry and thirsty, having to shout constantly. Polly felt the panic rising again as she looked above her head at the grasses tossing there, reaching toward the sky, closing in on her.

"Poo . . . lly! Where are you! Polly!" Jessie called.

Polly's mind had been lost in the web of grass stalks and rushes. She'd forgotten to call back.

"I'm coming back. Stay there. I'm coming now," Polly called.

20

The Call

The girls waited for dusk, too tired to talk, and listened to frogs and crickets starting up. Polly knew that out there on the prairie some strong, late summer wind was blowing. She could hear it always rustling through the seed heads above her. She wished it could come down through the slough grasses to cool them.

Jessie was sleeping, or trying to, but her constant shaking had started again. How long had it been? How long had they been lost? Three hours? Four? It seemed longer. She tried not to think about the pain from the broken blisters, the hunger, the thirst. And she was sick of the stench of the slough grass. She watched the grasses and tried to think about

Gus and Sammy and Helga and the calf. They'd be grazing now. With no one to watch them. Unless the Smiths had them. But if they did, when Papa came, they would all go to the Smiths' and get the animals back. And then the Smiths would see she had been right. They would see Papa had come back. And then she was asleep.

Polly awoke to the whimpering of Jessie. She sat up. It was night now. Some moonlight was filtering through. The clouds were moving out. Jessie was still trembling.

Polly got the canteen. It was not heavy anymore. Most of the water was gone. She gave Jessie a swallow and took one herself.

"It's cool now, Jessie. And I can see some. I'm going to look around again. Maybe our voices will carry farther now. It's so still."

"No," Jessie whined. "Not at night, Polly."

"I'm going, Jessie. One of us has to, and you have to call to me. Will you? Will you call to me?"

"Don't go," Jessie cried. "Don't leave me here. Let me go too. Let's just go together . . . please. Polleeeeee . . ." Her voice rose.

"No. You have to do what I say."

Polly left and moved slowly through the jumble of growth, through the heavy bunches of sedges and grass. She slapped at the tiny sting of something on her arm. She stumbled twice. The air was cooler and held the smell of rotting wood.

She had gone maybe a hundred feet when she stopped.

Something was out there.

Somewhere out there in the night, she heard something. Something far off. Not Jessie. Something from the other direction. "Jessie!" she shouted. "I'm stopping here. Do you hear me? Can you hear what I said?"

"Yes." The call came back.

"I think I heard something. I want to listen. I want you to be quiet until I call your name again. But I'm going to be calling out for help. Do you hear me?" The answer again from Jessie and then quiet.

Her heart was beating harder. She could feel it. The beating of her heart. The rising of her hope. There was something out there. She knew it and she listened. The air was cool and the night was a deep blue and Polly heard it again. Faint and distant. She couldn't tell what it was. Some kind of call.

Papa?

Maybe it was Papa.

Polly's heart was racing. Let him hear me. Let him, she prayed.

"Pa . . . paaa . . ." Polly screamed with all her strength.

She listened.

"Pa . . . paaaa . . ." And then she listened again and held her breath and there was nothing.

"Pa . . . paaaa . . . !" she called again and waited.

"Pa . . . paaa . . . !" There it was again! While she had been shouting. Intertwined with her voice, she had heard the call again. Papa?

She held her breath and waited.

And then she heard. Then she could make it out and it was the call of a coyote.

Just a coyote.

Not Papa.

Not even one of the Smiths coming to help.

A coyote.

She took a step backwards. Her feet sank in the damp soil and some leaves tickled her neck. Something like a horsefly blindly buzzed into her forehead but was gone before she could slap it aside.

The thought settled into her mind. It was not her papa.

She wondered if Jessie heard the coyote. She wouldn't say anything to Jessie. The coyote was miles away, it wouldn't come their way. She waited and later she heard it again farther away and then no more.

"Pooo . . . llllyyyyy . . ."

"Jee . . . ssie . . ." Polly stood there and called into the stillness.

Then a little louder until Jessie heard and called back.

"I'm coming back now . . ." Polly turned. Something whisked by her face, a slender grass leaf, and she swept it away and saw the stalks.

And these stalks had light behind them. The light of the moon.

For a moment she stood wondering, looking at the moonlight with clear black stalks outlined against it. She wondered for only a moment before she knew.

It *must* be the open prairie behind those outlines of stalks.

"Jessie!" she shouted. "I found something. . . . Bring the canteen and walk toward my voice . . . Jessie?" No answer. "Jessie, will you do that?"

"Yes."

So Jessie came and they went together toward the lighter blue and came out of the slough onto the wide open prairie, and they laughed because they could see the stars coming out and they could look straight ahead and see all the way to the hills. The soft night wind cooled their faces and necks and arms. It flapped their dresses against their legs, and Polly held her arms out and stretched her fingers open wide to feel it rushing by.

"There's a creek east of here," Polly said. "We can follow it right to the river."

Jessie took the canteen and opened it. She handed it to Polly. "One swallow," she said, and they laughed again.

Polly gave Jessie a big hug and grabbed the canteen and drank and then Jessie drank and there was no more.

"Let's rest awhile, I'm tired!" Polly laughed. She dropped to the ground and leaned back on her elbows. A nighthawk sailed over them into the starlight.

"Are we going back to the deer path? To our camp?" Jessie asked. "Without the compass?"

"When we get to the river up here, we won't be anywhere near the deer path. We'll be close to home. We can go there and eat . . . then we can decide what to do."

"Will we go tonight?"

Polly looked to the North Star, smiling. "Yes. And when we come to the river, we'll wait there till morning."

Polly knew they would have to find the river tonight. They needed water before the heat of the sun set in. She thought of the great blue heron lifting out of the slough and she knew they would get to the river tonight.

That night they walked in the cool, dark air under an open sky full of more stars than the world had room for. They walked in the shadowy moonlight and wondered if Sammy was chasing rats under the same moon.

21

The Soddy

$\mathcal{P}$olly just wanted to get home. Bone tired and thirsty, Polly didn't think further than that. So they walked. The blue prairie spread out to the stars and all around them the night grasses whished softly in the wind. They came to slough grasses again, rushes and cattails and cordgrass. And they knew they'd found the creek. Edging the water there in thin bands, the grasses were easy to get through even in moonlight. They followed the creek to the river and slept. Home was close now.

They left the river in the early light and before daybreak they stood on the ridge west of the soddy. Trails of little bluestem grew there. Polly didn't see them. She only saw the homestead. The wind whipped her hair into her face, into her eyes, and she pushed it away. Her worn linen dress popped back and forth below her knees and Polly started to run.

※※※

They found the soddy as they had left it. The door swung open now, though, the latchstring dangling in the wind. Helga and her calf grazed down near the creek, and Gus, closer, looked their way. Polly got water from the cistern and started potatoes cooking, and Polly and Jessie found new tomatoes and sat at the table and ate them.

Afterwards they splashed water on their faces from the rain barrel and changed into clean clothes and spotted Sammy near the stable before he dashed away. The sun grew warm. They dug in the garden and carried what they could salvage back to the soddy.

And then they heard the wagon.

It was still some ways off. They could hear it, though, and they went out in the wind carrying more fresh tomatoes in their hands. Their eyes followed the round lines of the prairie, the slopes and rises of the land. The Smiths would be coming from the east, from their homestead. There was nothing there. There was nothing anywhere. Just the rumble. And fear. And hope.

Polly saw a small blur, north, between the river and the rising sun. A wagon. Northeast.

"There . . ." she said, pointing. "Over there . . . see?"

They stood and watched. Jessie's hands went to her mouth. Polly squinted, held her hands up against the brilliance of the sun. The wagon kept coming, still more than a mile away but coming.

When it was closer and they could see it clearer, they saw there was one driver.

And a team of horses.

A team of horses, touched with the coral light of morning. . . . And they didn't say it out loud. But they knew in their hearts.

They knew.

It was Papa. They had known from the start it was Papa.

Polly raced through the corn, Jessie behind her, knocking the stalks aside with their arms, and through the oats and on out into the wild grasses, their feet burning and they did not care. Polly stumbled and fell and picked herself up, and Jessie caught up with her and stopped, gasping for air, and they stood watching that wagon.

Their papa was calling their names. He was calling their names across the wide prairie. They saw his hair shining in the sun when he took off his hat and waved it at them. And when he got closer, they could see his face.

And they ran again toward the wagon and the beautiful team of horses. They ran toward their papa who had come back.

Selected Bibliography

Butcher, Solomon D., and Harry E. Chrisman.
*Pioneer History of Custer County, Nebraska:
With Which Is Combined Sod Houses of the Great
American Plains.* Broken Bow, Neb.: Purcell,
[1976].

Costello, David F. *The Prairie World.* Minneapolis:
University of Minnesota Press, 1980.

Dick, Everett. *The Sod House Frontier 1854–1890:
A Social History of the Northern Plains . . .*
Lincoln: University of Nebraska Press, 1989.

Hofstadter, Richard, William Miller, and Daniel
Aaron. *The United States: The History of a Republic.*
Englewood Cliffs, N.J.: Prentice-Hall, [1967].

Jennewein, J. Leonard, and Jane Boorman, eds.
Dakota Panorama: A History of Dakota Territory,
Sioux Falls, S.D.: Brevet Press, 1973.

Madson, John. *Where the Sky Began: Land of the
Tallgrass Prairie.* Ames: Iowa State University
Press, 1995.

McIntosh, Charles Barron. *The Nebraska Sand Hills:
The Human Landscape.* Lincoln: University of
Nebraska Press, 1996.

Noll, Richard. *The Encyclopedia of Schizophrenia and the Psychotic Disorders.* New York: Facts on File, 1992.

Riley, Glenda. *The Female Frontier: A Comparative View of Women on the Prairie and the Plains,* Lawrence, Kan.: University Press of Kansas, 1988.

Riley, Glenda, ed. *Prairie Voices: Iowa's Pioneering Women.* Ames: Iowa State University Press, 1996.

Welsch, Roger L. *Sod Walls: The Story of the Nebraska Sod House.* Broken Bow, Neb.: Purcells, [1968].